THE BREACH

THE BREACH
Renato Prada

Translated by Walter Redmond

DOUBLEDAY & COMPANY, INC.
GARDEN CITY, NEW YORK 1971

THE BREACH was published in Spanish
by Editorial Los Amigos del Libro (Cochabamba–
La Paz, Bolivia) under the title *Los Fundadores del Alba*.

Library of Congress Catalog Card Number 70–135716
Printed in the United States of America
First Edition

CONTENTS

Proem   1

Part One   9

Part Two   43

Epilogue   145

TO MY WIFE, ELDA

PROEM

'Laura,' the man says.

'Yes, Father.'

'Do you hear any noise outside?'

'No; no I don't, Father.'

Their bodies touch in the darkness of the small house. The old man is trembling; the girl covers her mouth with her hand to hold back a scream. The hens start cackling in the coop; the dog is barking furiously. Seconds plod by like toads. Seas of sweat pour down the old man's body. Laura places her other hand on him soothingly. Their frightened eyes meet and turn away toward the well.

It was a nice day yesterday, but there was already something about the air. The old man said the air felt heavy, full of odd things that his lungs knew but his brains could only guess.

"Our lungs know more than our brains, because they

find out things in the air, out where the things themselves are. I knew it when you mother was going to die. My lungs told me plain, but my brains didn't want me to believe it, so they refused to. Until the neighbor came running up and his words started to wound my soul, down deep beyond my lungs and brains." The old man said it just yesterday.

They remember it now because their eyes are there to remind each other. Somebody has come into the yard. No mistaking the sound of footsteps. The dog whines with fear and scratches at the door of the house. Laura jumps up, grabs the machete, and rushes out. "My ears didn't want to believe it either, what my lungs knew all along." Laura trips over the dog scrambling to get inside, and stumbles forward in a wild dance, carving out crazy shapes in the air with the machete. Before she falls to the ground, a hand darts out from the shadows and grips her hand holding the machete. Laura wants to scream, but her tongue will not obey.

'Quiet, girl,' the man commands.

Startled, Laura climbs out of the river. She thought she heard a voice. She snatches up the dress lying on the bank and throws it over her naked body. Nothing stirs on the bank, not even a leaf on a tree.

The voice that went with the hand clasping her wrist told her to be quiet.

'Laura, get back in here before something happens to you. All they're doing is stealing the animals, that's all they're doing, Laurita. Don't stay out there; it's not worth it. Better come in here right away,' the old man calls from the house. Laura is frozen.

4

The girl looks around; nobody is there. Nobody could have seen her. She wants to run back to the house.

'We're only taking what we need, Miss,' says the voice. 'We're leaving you some money on the wall under a brick; get it when we're gone.'

The voice is reassuring. The hand is not hurting her. "It's the voice that spoke to me in the river," Laura says to herself. The hand gradually eases the pressure; now it no longer touches her skin, and the man has noiselessly vanished. Her father mutters something from inside.

'I'm coming Father,' Laura says.

"Don't be afraid," the man from the river told her. He holds her wrist, speaks in her ear. She wants to tell him: no, she isn't afraid, she wasn't afraid at the river when she knew he was watching her. When she opened her mouth to speak, the man was already gone.

'No, I didn't see anybody,' says Laura.

'You're lying,' says the Sergeant. 'Somebody was here last night. There's footprints. You can't fool us, honey. Both of you are covering for a bunch of dirty bandits. They robbed you. You shouldn't be afraid of them.'

"Don't be afraid," the voice at the river and in the night.

'I knew something like this was going to happen,' says the old man.

The Sergeant does not hear him; he orders the soldiers to turn everything inside out. Laura repeats mechanically that she hasn't seen anybody.

5

'They had already taken the animals by the time I got outside,' says Laura.

The Sergeant stares at her, picturing what is hidden behind the single fold of her thin dress.

'Got a nice-looking daughter, Grandpa,' he says. 'Keep her away from those bandits. Next time they're looking for meat they just might snatch this little chicken.'

The old man does not answer. "That day I saw the neighbor running up the path from the river, and I wanted to tell him don't shout because I already know. And then Laura comes up from the river with that funny look in her eye. Something else, I said to myself. I asked her what's wrong, and she didn't breathe a word; just floated by into the house and kept mooning around in the back," thinks the old man without noticing the Sergeant's leer.

Everyone knows the Captain's a tough bastard. He could probably go in the jungle by himself and clean up the guerrillas in ten minutes. Everybody's watching him strut around the plaza. He says, You should all know, the reason we're here's to enforce law and order. All the guys'd like to be like him, grow a bushy mustache and have a pot like that. He's out of shape, but it makes him look tough and sexy. The babes around here started drooling as soon as they saw him. He's telling them, Something else you should all know: this business has nothing at all to do with politics; those guerrillas are just a bunch of bandits robbing people and killing the helpless and—excuse the expression—screwing the women. The ol' Captain's really giving it to 'em, and the goddam sun is really killing us. The people are all crowded together in the middle of the plaza, scared shitless and nodding to everything the Captain yells.

We're sweating like sonsofbitches; it's like being in an oven. There's the mayor, a skinny little runt, all white and shaky. He's going over to the Captain to tell him something. The Captain says he has not finished his little talk and if His Honor would be so kind as to wait and all that crap. The walking corpse stays right there and scratches his head. Makes me feel sorry for the poor godforsaken sap; he must have a hard life. And nobody around here's going to protect those dirty bastards—pardon the French, ladies and gentlemen—because the High Command will consider it an act of treason against our Country. A glob of sweat as big as a grasshopper is crawling down my back headed for my ass. And no true Bolivian should stand by while those dirty . . . those dirty sonsofbitches—sorry, but let's call a spade a spade—deal his Country a foul blow. Parrot starts making slurpy noises like a thirsty dog and I tell him, Shut up, you dumb bastard, cuz if the Captain hears you it'll be your ass. For we Bolivians shall defend our Country, and nobody's pulling the wool over our eyes. The mayor actually squeezed out a couple of drops of sweat; I don't know where the hell he got them from, I'd swear he was as dry as a zombie in a Dracula movie. You may recall the example of Ignacio Wagner; that great patriot came from around here, like all of you. The Captain winds it up, but his pot keeps shaking in his pants like Jello. The rickety old mayor asks has the Captain finished now; Yes, I have; would Your Honor like to say a few words? We're sweated out to the last drop, wrung out down to the last damp spot in our soul. That goddam sun can really roast you when it wants to. And nothing's going to stop it.

8

PART ONE

Father Rector tells him to be seated and wait a moment while he finishes typing a letter. "The joys and hopes, the sadness and anguish of the men of our times, especially of the poor and suffering, are at the same time the joys and hopes, the sorrow and anguish of the disciples of Christ," reads the theology professor, raising his index finger and uttering each syllable with mystic delight. "That's all very true, but it doesn't mean the Church is all wrong," says Carlos, looking at him gently. "You're too good for your actions to be good . . . too good to act, I mean," replies Javier. The Rector cannot seem to find the word he wants; he rests his fingers on the keys of the typewriter and glances over at the young man. The two young men come into their room and sit facing each other. Javier notices that Carlos is pale. "It's a terrible decision to make," muses Carlos. Javier paces up and down in his room nervously. "There is nothing truly human that finds no echo in His heart." Javier rises and tells the professor he would like to ask a question. The priest lays his book aside; his look of beatitude has disappeared and is replaced by one of impatience. Carlos tells him he should pray harder, ask God for stronger faith. "Faith is a gift from God, and we must ask for it; we seldom remember to pray for more faith." The Rector says, "Come in." Javier still hesitates at the door, undecided. "Come in," repeats the Rector. "What are you trying to say, young man?" asks the professor. "We must be careful; the Church is not unjust, still less uncharitable. The bourgeois who do not practice charity and do not carry out their duties in justice are not the Church." "But, Father, they go to Mass and Communion, they rule the life of Catholic institutions." Javier cannot sleep, and he gets up out of bed. "I must carry out my decision once and for all," he thinks. The professor stares at him in surprise, one of his hands resting on the book left open before him. The two friends are alone in the room. He says, "You read, or do you want me to?" "If you want to." Javier sits down on the edge of the bed; his feet curl when they touch the cold tiles. Carlos sleeps peacefully. "The sleep of the just," Javier thinks. His steps echo in every bone. In the corridor the boys stop talking when they see Javier coming, and begin again after he passes by. Javier paces barefoot in his room. His knock on the door of the Rector's office sounds brusk. Carlos wakes up with a start. "I'm sorry," says Javier. Two loud knocks. The Rector pulls the paper out of his typewriter and begins to read it over, tilting his chair back. Javier halts before the Rector's office and looks back; the long hall seems to go on to infinity, losing itself in nothingness. The young men look at each other, their expressions frozen like cold, blank masks. Javier sits down on Carlos' bed. "Carlos, Carlos." "Hence the Church feels herself bound up intimately with the human race and its history." "I didn't mean to disturb you." The room is cold and shadowy, but Carlos' round, boyish face is visible. "Please repeat that," says Carlos. The professor is pale now. "Where is your common sense?" "Well now, what brings you in here, young man?" says the Rector without looking up from his letter. "For the Church encounters the world, the whole family of mankind, together with the entire gamut of reality wherein mankind is situated." Carlos stops reading and looks at Javier, who sighs and says he doesn't know what to think any longer, that everything's all confused. "It's a question of loving, Javier, not understanding," says Carlos. Javier looks out his window into the quiet, starry sky. Carlos' peaceful, rhythmic breathing is the only sound in the room. "But socialism, psychoanalysis, existentialism—aren't these doctrines part of this reality, of this gamut wherein mankind is situated?" asks Javier. Father professor reddens. "We have the encyclicals," he says. Carlos wakes up and looks at him in surprise. "My good friend." The Rector glances at the shelf laden with books and rubs his hand over his brow in a gesture of weariness and grief. "You have been considered the best student for the past six years," says the Rector. Small bulbs cast feeble circles of yellow light in the corridor, contorting the boys' faces into grotesque carvings. "Yes, Carlos, it

13

is indeed a question of loving, but love is a force that urges us to action. It's not a philosopher's love that can ease human sorrow, but the love of men who toil away at their daily lives." Carlos bows his head. The professor comes in smiling, carrying a big tome in his hands. "He's begun to pray," thinks Javier, looking at Carlos' bowed head. "The world, stage of human history, with all its yearnings, its failures and victories; the world that Christians believe is grounded and sustained by the Creator's love . . ." "But Father, don't you see that the Church is no longer in the world? The Church has condemned the world; it is still condemning the world. That's the first thing we learn: what's wrong with others, how people go wrong. Right here, every trace of the world has been erased, right within these seminary walls where we, the future salt of the earth, are living." "Yes, of course, Javier, I know your problem, but . . ."; the Rector falls silent, unable to hit upon the right word. Carlos looks up at him through eyes full of tears. "The thing that really breaks my heart is hurting you," says Javier, grasping Carlos' shoulder. "We're always taught one thing: where others go wrong. We have no hesitation about noting down all their mistakes in thought, word, and deed; we never make any mistakes." The day begins across the sky, hovering over the rooftops. The professor bangs his fist on his desk. "This is too much," he cries, "I cannot allow you to go on with such nonsense!" The Rector looks at him with studied compassion: "I think perhaps you're a little tired." The professor enters the classroom and glances around looking for Javier. He is absent. "Javier's not feeling well today," says Carlos. The

14

professor beams at the students, his eyes seeming to say, "Didn't I tell you something was wrong with him?" Carlos lowers his eyes. "Come on, Javier, let's read a little; it always makes us feel better and cheers us up." "There are some things whose explanations we should not seek, because there are none," says the Rector. Javier knocks at the door of the Rector's office and waits. "It's okay, Carlos, let me be by myself." "In our own days, the human race, amazed at its own discoveries and power, frequently asks itself anguished questions about the present evolution of the world, about man's place and mission in the universe, about the meaningfulness of his individual and collective efforts," reads the professor. Javier is alone in the room. He lies down on the bed and stares at the ceiling. Someone has stopped outside the door. Javier hears a few hesitant steps and thinks it may be Carlos, but it can't be, because he would walk right in. "You know, if you start out getting upset over everything, you will never be satisfied. . . . You now have a task before you, a very important one: to grow and mature in your intellectual and spiritual life. And by and by you will come to understand perfectly everything which now so scandalizes you." The professor sits down and begins to comment on the reading. Carlos thinks of Javier. Carlos embraces Javier and says he should think it over, because his decision is so overwhelming. "Our Christian spirit, the spirit of the Gospel," says the Rector. Javier takes the book and begins reading. "Read that verse over again," says Carlos. Father professor has stopped before Javier's door; he raises his hand to knock, but something stronger than his intention halts it in mid-air. "I'm staying in my room today; I won't go to class," says Javier. The professor drops his hand. "I'll speak with the Rector," he tells himself, and goes back the way he came. "Carlos, I've been thinking about this for months. You know I have." "I know," says Carlos, "but remember that it will change your whole life." "The Church is impelled by no earthly ambition. She desires but one thing: to carry on, under the guidance of the Spirit, the very work of Christ, Who came to the world to bear witness to the truth, to save and not to judge, to serve and not to be served." "And not to be served. And not to be served," Javier thinks. "Besides, you still lack sufficient preparation to be able to know and really understand the magnitude of the statements you're making in this classroom," says the professor, calmer now. "But when will I have that ability, Father? Why have we made things so complicated, and changed a religion of semi-illiterate shepherds and fishermen into a Greco-Roman institution, where theological niceties and legalistic hairsplitting seem to have become its essence?" The Rector raises his eyebrows in surprise. "My dear boy, my dear boy," says Father Rector. Carlos gets up from his bed and takes a few steps; he hangs his head, overwhelmed by sorrow. "A vacation perhaps, my boy?" The professor picks up his book and reads the passage again, this time without commentary. The atmosphere in the classroom is thick, uncomfortable. "A little rest is just what you need; it's good medicine for the soul when it gets a little run down," says the Rector. The two young men embrace; they look out the window at the dim patches announcing a new day. "It's the word of love,

Javier," says Carlos. "I'll tell the Rector right now, today, tonight," says Javier. Javier sits down beside Carlos. Nobody in the class speaks. "Father, I've been thinking it over for months." Carlos comes in at noon and says that the theology professor spoke to him and said he came, but could not bring himself to enter the room. "It is the human person whom we must save; it is human society that we must renew." Carlos begins to weep silently and grasps Javier's hand. Footsteps sound in the hall. Javier remains lying in bed, his eyes fixed on a pulsating spot on the ceiling. "A decision of this nature means a new direction in your life," says the Rector. The professor continues to read his text, and Carlos does not raise his head. The two friends embrace, leaving the book aside. "I'll be regretful for the rest of my life, because we'll never be again as we are now, as we've been," says Javier. "No, don't say that," begs Carlos. The room is light now, and from the broad patio of the Major Seminary floats the mellow, irksome call of the bell. "It is, consequently, man, but man as a whole, body and soul, heart and conscience, mind and will. . . ." Carlos reaches out and touches his friend's hand. Carlos. For man as a whole. Carlos.

The footsteps move off down the hall. Javier puts his magazine aside. "I'd be crazy to go through with it," he thinks. There is a moment of silence. "Don't do it, Juana," Javier says to himself. The girl stands at the end of the hall, her hand frozen on the light-switch. Her breathing comes as an effort. A board creaks under her feet; she starts and lowers her hand. The hall is dark. "I shouldn't do it," Juana tells herself. She tiptoes a short distance toward Javier's room. Her tense nerves cause her to tremble violently. "I really shouldn't do it," she repeats.

Javier picks up the magazine. "Sentenced to death," he reads, not particularly interested by the words. He is thinking about Juana, who should be out in the hall now. "The great Irish actor," he reads. He puts the magazine down and gets up. He looks at the picture of the condemned actor. A handsome man with an indifferent expression before the reporters' flash. He hears a noise in the hall. "Juana's out there; she's coming," he says to himself with a mixture of pleasure and misgiving. The girl has stopped again. "I really shouldn't do it." She is standing before the door of Javier's parents' bedroom. She wonders, what if the door opened and her employer's angry face appeared? What could she ever say to him? She wouldn't know what to do. Better think about something else: tomorrow's housework, or what she did today, or what Javier told her: "I'll be waiting for you in my room tonight; I want you to come." The veins in her temples seem about to burst. She wishes Javier would come out to rescue her. She begs him to come out. "Javier, you know I'm out here," she thinks fiercely. Someone said something in the parents' room. Her legs start shaking and start to give way. The hall has never looked so long and horrible.

Javier looks at the picture of the gay-sad actor, the "one-time idol of the crowds who are now bitterly receiving the news of his condemnation." The actor looks gallantly out at him from the magazine. "Juana, you shouldn't come tonight," he thinks. "Poor Juana; please, you don't have to come."

In the hall, Juana prays Javier will open the door to save her the embarrassment of doing it herself. She takes three bold steps. Javier's parents' room is behind her at last, but she hears them talking again. She thinks she heard the father say something like "Be still" or "I'm sleepy" or maybe "I'll speak"; then the woman's voice: "He must be suffering, too," or perhaps "He doesn't seem to realize," or something like that. Juana is now at

Javier's door. She leans her cheek against the cold wood and strokes it with the palm of her hand. A tear of weariness, of shame, of happiness, runs down her face to her neck and is lost. "God, now what if he doesn't want me to come?" she asks herself. "Could he have changed his mind from this morning?" From the parents' room a louder exchange has come, like an argument, and died out immediately in the silence.

Javier is lying in bed again. He has picked the magazine up and goes on reading. "When the unhappy actor was notified by his doctor about the state of his health and advised . . ." Juana's hand rests on the doorknob; it feels cold and she pulls back momentarily. "He said, almost smiling: I've already got my epitaph worked out." The doorknob moves soundlessly; Javier can see it slowly turning. He continues reading what the actor went on to say: "God, what a shame!" Javier gets up and walks over to Juana, who is now pressed against the doorpost, pale, afraid to take another step, gazing at some point beyond Javier, beyond all possible things. Her hand still grasps the doorknob. The light from the room casts the shadow of a formless monster into the hall. "I'm glad you came," whispers Javier, as he takes her hand, still clutching the knob. "You weren't waiting for me," the girl says. Her hand will not let go of the doorknob. Javier fondles her fingers as he slowly pries them loose.

He closes the door. Juana feels calmer now and looks at the magazine lying on the floor. "I was reading," says Javier, just to say something.

Juana does not answer; she sits down on the edge of the bed. She is uncomfortable, not knowing what to do with her hands or where to turn her head. Javier sits down beside her and takes her hands in his. "Juana," he says, bringing his mouth to her ear, "you finally came." The girl lowers her head. Javier puts his arms around her and forces her back on the bed. "You told me to come," she says. Javier thinks of the unfortunate actor sentenced to die, to leave this our only life. He kisses the girl. Juana looks at him and gently pushes him away. "Javier, it's not right," she says. The young man stiffens and stares at her. A flicker of indecision crosses his eyes for the barest instant. She stands up and sighs. "Turn off the light," Javier tells her. "No; I don't know if it's all right," says Juana, almost in a tone of lament. Javier looks at her, then stands up and grabs her by the waist, pulling her over to the light-switch. "I'll get it, Juana honey," he says as he kisses her. The girl takes his hand and holds it against her. Their faces blur into a dark shadow, and their bodies stumble across the room to the bed.

Javier looks at his father, who is still trembling, open-mouthed, in the doorway. His mother runs toward him crying, "Stop! Don't. . . ." He stands in the street with nothing, without even a penny in his pockets. It is wintertime, and the morning is cold. "You're my son and not just some nobody," says his father, getting up from the table and throwing his napkin down on his plate. Javier watches the cloth getting wetter and wetter until it finally sinks completely into the soup. "Calm down, Son," begs his mother. Some passers-by stare at him in surprise; Javier feels them stop to turn around and snigger. "Dad, I can't go on living like this." "I don't know what you're talking about." "Let's finish our soup before it gets cold," says his mother. "But Mom, I have to let him know. I can't go on; it's just not right." His mother hugs him, shaking her head in disagreement. "Do it for me, will you?" A group of boys even point at him and start whispering and giggling. His mother has come into his room; she stares at him but cannot speak. "My clothes must look funny, or maybe my face," thinks Javier as he starts across the Parkway. His mother takes his hand. Javier stops and decides to cross the Parkway and go down España Street. The napkin turns a dull cream color. "It's prettier than when it's dry," Javier thinks. His mother looks into his eyes but cannot utter a word. He toys with a lock of hair. His father has come into the dining room. The tension on his face turns his usual radiant smile into an artificial grin and shows he is expecting something. "Don't do it now, not yet," whispers his mother to him, taking his hand. Javier closes the door of his room and begins to change clothes. "I tell you I just can't understand him." Javier goes toward the gate and puts out his hand. Juana comes in with the soup and greets her employer. The man hardly answers. "First you want to enter the seminary. After a big argument, your mother and I had to give in. What else could we do? I knew you wouldn't make it; you didn't have the makings of a priest. But I said okay. It was 'the call of God,' your vocation. . . ." Javier sits down on a bench in the plaza Barba de Padilla. It is a small plaza but it means a lot to Javier. It brings back memories of his childhood; he can still see himself running and playing on the swings that are not there any more. Two boys go by and start laughing when they see him. Javier gets up from the bench, irritated. Juana glances at him out of the corner of her eye as she serves his soup. Javier has not told her anything about his plans. He feels guilty when he sees how dejected she is. He walks over to the

24

stand. "It'll be the last straw for the old man," he says to himself. "Second, you come home without even telling us to expect you. Okay, your vocation's over. I'll forget everything. I don't hold anything against you. Your mother and I are happy to have you back. You can start all over again." Javier hears footsteps approaching his door. The door opens. Javier touches the gate; the metal feels cold. "Javier," says his mother, "you'll die like an outlaw." Javier looks scornfully around the room he used to think so inviting. "At least let him eat his lunch in peace. You know how tired he comes in." "Tired from what?" "From the big responsibility of running a company." "I just wish that once, just once, he'd have the responsibility of not being able to bring home any bread." "These ideas of yours. . . ." "So how's your dad, Don Javier?" asks the man. "Here's your carton of smokes." "Thanks . . . he's okay. . . ." "Don't worry about it, Don Javier." "You can't blame anybody for being born rich if he keeps on doing well on his own; actually . . ." "Don't worry about it, Don Javier, I'll just charge it up to your dad." "But I've decided to do something different with my life. I don't want to be a boss just because I inherit a company." His mother looks at him and presses her cheek to his; her eyes look tired and swollen. "I don't want to lose you," say her sad eyes, piercing deeper than her words. In the street Javier remembers his mother's look. "Pain and sacrifice is the price I have to pay," he says to himself. "You get those ideas from those kids you run around with and all those damn books you read," his father said, now pale with anger. He opens the closet and picks out his oldest and shabbiest clothes.

"Don Javier, I know it's none of my business, but I think your clothes . . ." As he arrives at the foot of the stairs he sees his father standing in the middle of the hall, his hands on his hips. "Third, you're going to study Sociology. And nobody says a word to you. But then you start reading those damn books, written by people sick with hatred, and keep coming out every now and again with those wisecracks of yours. I won't change my mind. I think you'll get over it as you'd get over a fever." Javier looks at the clothes he's got on: old khaki pants, a red shirt, and a blue jacket from high school that is too short in the sleeves. "So that's what's making them laugh." He smiles to himself. His mother's head appears over his father's shoulder. Neither says a word. Javier edges by, barely touching them. His mother bursts out crying. "Leave him alone; he'll be back; eggheads don't know how to work," says his father, preventing his wife from rushing after Javier. Javier comes to the door and reaches out his hand. He hears a sob. He looks around and there is Juana, behind his father, standing forsaken in the middle of the hall, chewing the corner of her apron. Javier gives the doorknob a hard twist. "I get it; you're doing it on a bet, right, Don Javier?" asks the man in the stand. España's as quiet as any other street. Better go down Veinticinco de Mayo Street to the end to pick up José, and then we'll catch a truck for La Paz. "No, Mother, really; it's not just another whim," he says. "It's more than that; it's something I have to do, something I've felt called to do right from the start." "You said the same thing when . . ." She breaks off, not wanting to say anything that would hurt him. The cold morning air strikes his face as he jerks the door open. "Poor Juana," he thinks. He looks at his room for the last time and walks into the hall.

"So you finally got here," says José. "Let's go, man, we don't have any more time to lose." "How about a meat pie, Don Javier?" "No, thanks, I'm sort of in a hurry." When the man insists, Javier accepts in order not to offend him. "I used to raise a lot of hell, too, in the old days, Don Javier. Once I bet the guys I'd walk into the plaza dressed like an indian woman. At that time, you know, Cochabamba wasn't a fifth as big as it is today; the Parkway barely existed." "I'll say good-by to Babe. Want to come in or wait?" says José. "I'll wait." "So there I was, Don Javier, I had to do it. Well, I walked all the way to the plaza in my mother's indian skirt. When I got there you can imagine what happened." José stops after a few steps; his eyes have filled with tears. "She's going to start crying again, poor thing," he says; "she cried all night." Juana chews her pink apron and looks at him, unable to say a word. "Now he's bitching about the right to private property, and . . ." "Don't use language like that," his mother pleads. The father stands up furiously. "You can't talk at all in this place any more!" he shouts. "And all those little shits, pardon the expression, Don Javier, running behind me and yelling stuff like: 'Hey lookit that dark meat,' and 'She looks like a good rassle,' and I don't know what else." José raises his hand to his forehead. "I guess she'll understand. I told her it's for the future of our Country, for our children, for us, too. . . . It's not easy, is it, man?" says José. Javier grips his shoulder in sympathy. The two young men set out for Aroma Avenue. Juana hangs her head as Javier's father leaves his wife and goes to the door Javier has left open. "So this drunk hears it and comes over to us and starts getting horny over me, pardon the expression, Don Javier. Then they all take off and leave me alone to stand off the drunk. He starts grabbing for me and tells me we're going to bed and he's got something real nice to show me." Javier waits opposite José's house. In this neighborhood his clothes cause no surprise. His father stands in the doorway looking out at him with a scornful smile. Javier opens the gate. The street is almost deserted; it is cold. After walking a bit, he pauses to decide what streets he'll take to the Market neighborhood. "And then the creep actually starts trying to feel me up, Don Javier. Naturally, I can't call the cop standing in front of the governor's office. Finally I can't take it any more, and I slug him and tell him to get the hell outta there in my regular voice. The guy staggers back from the punch and blinks his eyes, surprised-like. Blood's coming out of his nose." The man in the stand bursts out laughing. "Yeah, Javier, it hurts all right," José says. Javier looks at him with affection. Babe has come out to the doorway, her two children clutching her skirt in dismay over their mother's tears. She has raised the corner of her apron to her mouth and bites it in helplessness and despair. Juana's face can no longer be seen in the hall; Javier's father's body blocks the door and hides everything inside. Babe and Juana understand nothing; they chew their aprons

28

and weep. Javier's father standing in the doorframe starts to raise his fist but lowers it at once; he says nothing. His mother runs past him out of the hall and cries, "Stop!" Javier must soon decide what streets he'll take to the Market neighborhood.

Their descent came to an end in the last of the Kingdom's chambers [beforehand, they had to pass through the fourth and fifth circles. Javier was at the moment playing Vergil in this strange drama, but he was soon to lose the role of teacher-guide, while José, the pupil-follower, was beginning his Vergilian metamorphosis, eventually to don the Master's olive branch and even gain his bearing; for as they drew near the city, Javier was still the one who answered and José the one who asked]. "Sit down, comrade," HE said, extending his hand [before, it was José's hand that was extended, his finger pointing to the mighty white mountains thrust up before them. Javier looked at Mount Illimani and explained all he knew to his friend and told him to keep his eyes shut until he said to open them. The train rumbled on monotonously across the Altiplano, coming at last to the end of the long journey]. Javier answered yes, he and his comrade had just arrived the night before. HE looked over the men sitting beside HIM and smiled so openly and pleasantly that Javier wondered how a person with such a candid, natural expression could bear the responsibility of such an enterprise. José [the man who knew more than anyone, more than Javier, what it meant to carry out this deed (the greatest deed of his life, the only deed that could make him feel he was somebody in this life) because (Javier knew this) it could not have been easy to leave his wife (that poor, almost unnoticed woman whom he, José, would call "Babe," and whom Javier hardly knew. Actually, Javier remembered seeing her twice: first when José, excited about Javier becoming a new Party member, invited him home and introduced her to him with the joy that a child must feel when he shows his playmate a secret toy that is all his. Javier shook her hand and wondered how this limp, fragile hand could possibly belong to a woman who did the hardest housework and in addition worked in a textile factory with her husband . . .)] asked HIM a question that Javier did not catch in his excitement. HE conferred in a low voice with HIS comrade sitting beside HIM before answering. Then HE spoke, becoming silent again almost at once, and flashed another of HIS engaging smiles. Everyone was staring at Javier. It still had not dawned upon him that he had to answer. He did not know what to say, and glanced over at José. His comrade motioned to him to speak up, but Javier could not even guess at the meaning of the words he had heard. Then HE looked away and called upon somebody else, to give Javier more time. Javier could still hear the last word of HIS question, hovering in

his ear like a tiny feather in a silent temple: "decision."
Someone emerged from the darkness into the yellow
light and broke the spell. Then Javier heard the clinking
of china. "Coffee," HE said. A hand [like Babe's, who
also had offered Javier a cup of coffee that first time he
met her, which he quickly accepted to put the family
more at ease, for they could think of nothing else to offer
the bourgeois young man] placed a steaming cup beside
the Chief. Javier said yes. It felt as if he had to squeeze
his rasping voice up through his throat, because [he
knew] that single syllable, actually even a simple nod of
his head would be enough, was deciding the whole future
of his life. "Fine," HE said, and motioned to one of the
comrades to take over on the details. The hand broke
into the circle of light and placed a cup of coffee next to
Javier. José smiled at him across the little, smoking cup
[. . . and the second time she couldn't even offer him a
cup of coffee, because Babe was doing all she could to
hold back the sorrow filling her eyes, as she watched the
father of her children leave their home and all the things
they had managed to gather in it, for the sake of something she did not understand]. The man filled them in
on all the details they asked about and smiled con-
tentedly as he fell silent. José got up and walked over to
the corner to have a smoke. Javier asked a few more
questions and then went over to join him. "Want a cigarette?" José asked. Javier did not answer; he stared at
him with eyes that glowed like coals in the darkness.
"We'll be going to different units," he said. "Yeah," said
José, putting the cigarette into his mouth and leaving it
there. Javier asked him for a drag. José handed him the

33

cigarette mechanically. Javier inhaled the warm smoke. "We should have been prepared for it," José said, placing his hand on his friend's shoulder. José closed his eyes [not as he did in the train, with that childish expectation Javier thought was so funny, not only because of the way he pressed his eyelids together, as if for fear they'd suddenly pop open against his will and rob him of the pleasure of surprise he would get when Javier told him to open them, but mostly because of the way he kept his mouth closed (Javier smiled again as he remembered it) by sucking in his lips like a blind, toothless elf] only to open them with a kind of resignation [although now this expression of simple resignation (which resignation was powerfully supported by the firm conviction that he was serving his ideal, serving what was greater than himself, his family, and Javier all together) was a far cry from his expression of surprise and childlike glee when he saw (after Javier ordered him to open his eyes), almost at his feet, the sparks twinkling merrily in what is the most dazzling hole in the Altiplano] and utter a word whose homeland is the realm of the Circle of Circles: "Social Justice."

Javier thinks how beautiful it is to recall the image of Vergil and Dante, hand in hand, guiding one another over the rugged path through the shadowy passages [circles] of this world [a world lacking nothing the other one enjoys: cerberi, effigies, gorgons, and even mournful sirens]. "Justice." Javier's voice repeats the word mechanically.

I'm not squeamish or anything, but hell, standing in line
bare-ass, waiting for the doc to check you out, well it's
sort of humiliating. The doc says quit bitching, everyone's getting his turn. He says I should open my mouth
and stick my tongue out. He looks at his assistant and
asks him if that's Colonel Cadima coming, while my
mouth's still open and my tongue's getting dry hanging
out there in the cold air. The doc says okay, I can pull
it back in now and shut my mouth. What do you have to
hang your tongue down to your chest for, and then he
just glances at it like it was an old hunk of meat? All this
is going through my mind. The doc says, Take a deep
breath and hold it until I say. Then he sees Colonel Cadima coming over and starts smiling and says to him over
his shoulder he's sorry he can't shake hands, and all the
time I'm holding my breath and dying for air. The
Colonel sees me strangling and asks, What's this recruit

doing cuz he looks purple and half gagged. The doc laughs and explains, It's because the recruit was ordered to take and hold a deep breath and hasn't been told to let it out yet. The Colonel says, I bet this man is going to be a fine soldier; his clammy fingers are on my shoulder, and I can hear the other guys laughing it up back in line. Okay, says the doc, next; and I go past the line to the dentist in the corner, with my balls flapping in the breeze.

The dentist is smoking and telling the sergeant about the guerrilla rumors. They're being spread by the enemies of our democratic regime to get the people all worked up, Sergeant. Right sir, says the sarge. You can't please anybody any more in this Country with all those damn commie revolutionaries around. Right sir. What this Country needs more of than anything else is law and order and hard work. Right sir; looks like that's the extent of the idiot's vocabulary. The chill from the floor's been creeping up my leg; it's up to my knees now, and I've got chickenskin all over. Great, me freezing my ass off and the sarge and the dentist shooting the shit. Must think a guy's made out of iron. And the sarge keeps on with his right sir. So then he says my teeth are all right cuz my face looks okay, and calls the next guy. How about that; I didn't even get to open my mouth. My teeth are supposed to be okay cuz my face's okay.

So I'm getting dressed; I'm in the army now and might as well forget about going anywhere for a while. We're up shit's creek, I tell the guy next to me. He looks at me and says, Without the proverbial paddle. He seems like a nice guy, the type who might turn out to be a good

buddy; that's what you need in a hole like this. I agree
with him and tell him my name and we shake hands.
He says, Call me "Parrot," that's what all my friends call
me. Army life is a drag and furthermore it's a crock of
shit, he says. I just keep agreeing with him and repeating what he says but not bitching or wising off on my
own. Parrot goes on talking; he says, That's one reason
why they call me Parrot, and also because of my nose,
and he points to it. But he can be a friend. He says I look
like a nice plain guy, not a bullshitter like some others.
At least I'm dressed now and not freezing my balls off.
Parrot's putting on a jacket with a big emblem of a Yankee
university on it; the jacket's yellow and the emblem is
blue with English writing. Parrot figures what I want to
ask and says, Anyone can buy one, but don't bother,
they're going to give us uniforms. "Anyhow, girls like
uniforms better." He winks and licks his lips. I tell him
what the dentist was saying about the guerrillas and ask
him if they're going to send us after them to defend our
Country. Parrot says, If they're pissing on you, they
might as well crap on you too. We laugh and shake hands
again and make some plans for Sunday, cuz Parrot knows
some nice-looking babes who are built and willing to put
out. So I tell him, Parrot baby, you and me's got a great
future.

One of them's Albertina, but they call her Tina; the other's Tere, or Teresa. Both of them are stacked and got nice hips. Tere says she'd just like to go to the show, but Tina thinks it'd be great to get something to eat and go dancing and just have a good time. Parrot knows where his bread is buttered, and he gives me a dirty wink and says, that's the best idea Tina's had in her whole life, ain't that right? I side with Tina and Parrot. So Tere loses by a large majority and has to obey orders from the High Command, squawks the Parrot. We're all laughing, and Parrot and I grab our girls by the waist and take off.

The bar's really swinging. The blackboard hanging outside with the menu written on it would make you drool just stopping to look at it. Lots of *chicha*, too, a drink for the drinking man, as Parrot puts it. He lets go of Tina's waist and dives into the bar like a fish into water. I'm holding Tere's hand and make like a poet and tell her, You know you look like a pretty red flower in that nice dress you got on. She says, Oh, you're just giving me a line.

The music's really going, and everybody's dancing and laughing. Parrot says, Have another drink, Tina honey. No, I've had enough, Parrot; everything's starting to look like it's made out of rubber. She slurs the words like they were made out of rubber, too. Okay, Tina baby, he says, let's go dance some more and sweat it off; the ol' Parrot's squawking away. I tell Tere to excuse me a minute, and she guesses what the excuse and the minute are for. I'm weaving around and can't quite seem to get my feet on the floor; it's always lower than where they want to go. And my steps are too short or too far to one side from where I want to put them down. Outside, the open door of the crapper is tilted; it's dark and still and looks like it's pushing up the tin roof hanging down from the sky filled with pretty stars. As I go into the room, I seem to be stepping down lower than in a regular room; the floor doesn't want me to walk on it, and when I try, it gets mad and pulls away. I bump into a guy coming out with his hand on his fly. He hiccups his Sorry, soldier. That's all right, I say, actually I'm the one who should say sorry, excuse me please, I'm terribly sorry. No, it's quite all right, as he finishes zipping up his pants and leaves.

Here I am pissing away in the trough; I was really busting a kidney cuz I drank so much. A nice, long piss; you can't see it in the dark. Feels tremendous cuz it was hurting pretty bad back there sitting with Tere. Feels nice and warm. Tere; I bet she's back there trying to

40

picture what I'm doing, right, Tere? Let's go; that's all of it, down to the last drop. Boy, Tere, that's one hell of a relief. Now to zip up fast and get back to you, Tere. Shit, where the hell'd the floor go again so I can get out of here. There you go, steady, that's it, take it easy, out we go to the music and the lights.

The singer's singing he'll wait his whole life no matter what for whoever the hell he's waiting for; his voice is all hot and bothered. Back at the table Tere's shaking her head and saying something to a guy who's trying to grab her arm; my blood starts boiling and I start moving over there. Parrot leaves Tina go and hits the bastard on the shoulder. Get your goddam hands off me, says the guy, and the singer says, though you may not remember me. Who the hell do you goddam soldiers think you are? I get over to him and punch him in the kisser. No one's cutting in on my Tere. There's a big commotion, the women shrieking, the music playing, and the Parrot squawking away. I'm saying, No fucking sonofabitch is going to fool around with my date; just try it again! And all this is just a going-away party, a send-off, cuz day after tomorrow we're moving out to do our duty, moving out to fight for our Country.

PART TWO

'Death is first of all a nice down payment on our wishes,' says Chaco, 'like selling our mind something on credit.'

The flames leap up, dancing joyously. All the other comrades in the camp are asleep.

'You think about death a lot,' says Javier.

Chaco smiles and throws a dry stick into the fire; it blazes up.

The sounds of combat come from the hillside. The sun seems to have stopped in its course over the battle. Its blinding rays thwart every attempt to see the spot where the Chief is pointing.

'Must be an army patrol,' says the Chief.

'Do we have to change our plans?' asks Darío.

'I think of death when I'm alone,' says Chaco; then he adds, 'when I feel all alone.'

'Alone,' echoes Javier.

The jumbled song of the insects and the black of the

thick forest, which blend only at night, hedge the camp on all sides.

'Do you have a girl?' asks Chaco.

'No, I don't have anybody either.'

Javier thinks of Juana. A flicker of joyless passion to warm one night. Ashes already? Probably, for poor Juana.

'Let's pick up everything and hide the food and ammunition,' orders the Chief.

'Right,' says Darío, and gets busy.

Each man moves to his assigned place to carry out the task he has performed many times. There is no confusion.

'We have to break camp,' says Javier.

'Where'll we go?' says Jerónimo.

'Farther back into the jungle,' Chaco tells him.

'Talking?' says the Chief, coming close to the fire.

'Yes, Chief,' answers Chaco, beginning to stand up.

'We took one prisoner; the rest are dead,' one of the men reports.

'That's bad news,' says the Chief.

The soldier keeps his hands raised. He watches the Chief with a look of curiosity and fear. His trousers are torn, and his shirt hangs open.

'They were armed,' the man speaks again.

'You can put your hands down,' the Chief tells the prisoner.

The soldier shakes his head and seems to wonder if he has heard rightly. He turns, looking at everybody standing around him in a circle. He seems to want to get a last look at everything before getting shot. His uneasy eyes shift back and forth, full of tears.

'He says to put your hands down,' repeats Chaco with a smile.

The soldier obeys. He stares down at his shoes, like a stubborn child. His hair is messed up.

'Bring him a cup of hot coffee,' the Chief tells Whitey, the Negro cook, who has also come over to see the prisoner.

'At ease,' says the Chief, sitting down beside the fire. 'I couldn't sleep,' he adds with an apologetic tone.

'We were talking about personal things,' says Chaco, 'about what we think of when we're alone.'

'It always makes us feel better to get things off our chest to a friend,' says the Chief.

The fire lights up the faces of the three men, creating new sets of features with its every movement. The Chief's beard juts out from his pale face of living rock.

'Chief, have you ever wondered about the meaning of your life itself?' asks Chaco, with keen interest.

'We weren't planning on attacking anybody. And we didn't expect to be ambushed like that,' says the soldier. 'They told us we were out on patrol to catch some dope smugglers. . . . You killed the whole patrol.' He tries to overcome the emotion that at times causes his voice to break. His body trembles. The cook hands him a cup of steaming hot coffee.

'Don't you see that we had to do it?' says Darío.

The soldier noisily slurps his coffee. From habit, he wipes imaginary sweat from his brow.

'The sorrow of those who came through can't see anything,' he says in a flat voice, uttering the words from deep within.

47

Nico didn't come back today. We have an idea things didn't go too well in town. The Chief orders a detail to watch the slope. Nico went to town to meet the contact from La Paz and buy some food. He left in a jeep like always, and he left at the same time as always. In town they think he's a rich, eccentric rancher who puts screwy messages on the radio and always has a pile of books. We were waiting the whole day on a rise on the slope from where you can see the road from town. "It could be pretty serious," said the Chief when we came back; he was worried. We didn't start a fire that night during the watch. It's better to be on the safe side.

'The revolution has been the meaning of my life for the past fifteen years,' says the Chief, stirring up the coals in the fire with a dry stick. He takes out a pack of cigarettes and offers them to the other two, and lights them up with the glowing tip of the stick. He blows out the first lungful of smoke and adds, 'Before that, I was the rebel son in a bourgeois family.'

Javier stares at him.

'In my thinking I've tried out all the roads,' he says; 'I've been practically everything I possibly could have been.'

The soldier's face is rough and swarthy. He has the protruding cheekbones and sunken eyes of an Aymara Indian.

'Well, when you came out here with weapons, you were running the risk of being attacked by the dope smugglers,' says Darío, determined to keep the conversation going with the prisoner.

'Yeah, but you shouldn't kill us by sneaking up on us,' retorts the soldier without ceasing to sip his hot coffee.

'This is one mission that cannot be detained for any reason,' says the Chief.

The prisoner finishes sipping the hot liquid. He gives his cup back to the cook, who remains standing in the circle, the cup in his hand.

'Then go ahead and kill me, to finish your mission,' he says, and makes the sign of the cross.

'Your whole life,' says Chaco with admiration, 'placed at the service of the cause.'

The men standing in the circle shoot questioning glances at each other. There is a moment of uncomfortable silence. The prisoner remains in the center, resigned to anything. He pulls a dirty handkerchief out of his pocket and blows his nose.

'Excuse me,' he says afterward.

'You're from the Altiplano,' says Jerónimo.

'Yes, sir. Now I'm serving my Country.'

'You're not serving your Country,' shouts Darío, 'just a bunch of capitalist puppets!'

Nico jumped into the jeep, smiled, and waved good-by to the Chief and the rest of us.

'Give my regards to the local wenches,' Darío called.

'I'll give it to them all right,' said Nico, and started the engine.

My eyes are getting tired from watching the horizon for the dust cloud that will announce Nico's return. The glaring rays of the sun shine into my eyes. "Not a sign of him," I'm thinking.

49

The Chief stretches out his legs and yawns. 'I'm getting sleepy again,' he says.

'But how about death, Chief?' Chaco asks again, with the same zest he puts into all his questions.

The departure is organized in a few minutes. The prisoner sits blindfolded beneath a tree. Everybody has a heavily loaded pack to carry.

'Nico didn't get back today. I'm afraid they've found out something. We'll have to start thinking about breaking camp at a minute's notice and holing up in the jungle. That way, the liberation campaign will gain a few months,' says the Chief, and adds, 'I've ordered six men to watch the slope. If an army reconnaissance patrol comes, it'll have to come through there. Their orders are to stop them.'

'Did you go to school?' asks Jerónimo.

'I know how to read and write. I studied in a country school run by some missionaries,' says the prisoner. He is a short man with a big chest and a thick neck.

We moved out. Our plans have radically changed after our ambush of the army patrol. We all know that the preparation period is gone forever and that our guerrilla action has begun.

'Death is an event that will always catch us off guard,' says the Chief. 'When that moment comes, I only hope I shall have done what it was my duty alone to do.'

Chaco blinks, puzzled, and stands up to throw some pieces of dry wood on the fire.

'I don't think we'll ever deserve death, any death,' he says after sitting down again.

The Chief gets up and yawns.

'It's pleasant sitting by a warm fire and talking, comrades, but sleep's overcoming me. I'm sorry,' he says, and walks back to his hammock. The Chief always sleeps out in the open.

'Good night, comrades,' he says from the hammock.

The men look at each other uncomfortably. The Chief steps forward.

'We don't intend to kill you,' he says. 'We'll set you free when we leave the camp.'

'Thank you, sir,' says the soldier. His voice is clear now, but its tone reveals neither surprise nor gratitude.

'The Chief's a tremendous guy,' says Chaco. 'He lives the cause with all his might, and he doesn't have any time for nonsense, like I do.'

"Nonsense, Chaco?" Javier thinks as he stretches out on the ground on his back to see the starry sky: an endlessness of silent stars sending down their light to earth forever, fromever, caught in an atom of time by the eyes of a mortal who grasps them all and who alone wonders in this infinite loneliness: "What's nonsense, Chaco?"

Then the Captain kicks the dog in the ass; well, what the hell, I guess he's supposed to know what he's doing. We watch the poor thing yelp and limp away to the end of the patio, and then it starts howling like it didn't have a friend in the world. Our eyes say what we're thinking, that it's not the poor mutt's fault those damn reporters come in here sticking their nose in the guerrilla thing, which is the army's business. The Captain lies down in the hammock, takes out a pack of cigarettes, and starts puffing away like he was really pissed off. He glares at anyone who happens to wander into range. We all find something to do to keep from catching his eye. There's always the dog; so I latch on to the dog to stare at. The thing that's fucking us up isn't so much having to fight the guerrillas as not having anyone to fight, cuz they disappear like magic, and it's one hell of a job going out there in the jungle carrying a rifle and trying to meet them man to man and have a showdown so we can get the damn thing over with once and for all. The Captain calms down after his third cigarette in a row. Things are looking up; he even seems to be feeling sorry for the dog; actually it's not like him to make something suffer just for the hell of it. I'm about ready to go over and pet the dog to give him an example of kindness to animals, when in from the street comes another one of those damn reporters from the city with so much time on their hands to be down here, as if the guerrillas were the only news now. The Captain's sore and says, Well I'll be a sonofabitch, under his breath so the reporter can't hear. He's already taking pictures of us, and we're hurrying up trying to straighten up our uniforms and turn on a smile. The Sergeant tells us to fall in and come to attention right away over where the Captain and the reporter are smiling at each other and introducing themselves; and he says, Be damn careful, we don't want any asshole shooting off his mouth, cuz if you do, the shit'll really hit the fan.

The Captain's giving the reporter his little speech, but it's not as fancy and snappy as the one he gave when we first came to town. The Captain's a man who knows how to rise to all occasions. The Sarge says, Okay, at ease, men, take it away Cap . . . you may now commence, Captain, sir. The Captain glares at him like he's going to bite his head off. We're figuring he didn't like that phoney "commence" business.

We loyal citizens of our Country have come here to struggle against the foreign invaders, says the Captain, his finger pointing straight at Parrot. The reporter breaks

54

in, I beg your pardon, Captain, but I don't know if you can really characterize the guerrilla action as foreign, since there are certain elements lacking which . . . And the Captain cuts him off, Well, actually there do exist those elements which you members of the press naturally cannot acknowledge for sound policy reasons obviously and out of respect to our Country's National Defense Forces. We're praying he'll get it over with, cuz the reporter's through taking pictures of us to print in his paper back in the city. The reporter says he's going to ask us a few questions, and the Captain bites the lip his mustache is riding on. He smiles and says that we may reply freely and the reporter should make himself comfortable so he can listen and the Sergeant should bring him a chair right away. That's quite all right; don't bother. By all means, the National Defense Forces are here to serve. So the Sarge runs out and comes back with a chair and the friendly smile you see in the Colgate ads. He puts the chair down, and the reporter sits down with his notebook in his hand, and looks us over slowly. And we all look at the Captain, pleading for help. His belly's shrunk back in the face of the threat of this guy grilling us. The reporter's pasty little face goes with his assignment; you can see how sneaky he is from his bulging eyes and his smirky little mouth. I'm thinking of the dog again; it's not howling any more. It's probably sniffing around the dirty pots in the kitchen. The Captain asks the reporter to please repeat his question and me to please answer. I feel the ground giving way under me and I open up my eyes as wide as they go to make my face come to attention. The words of his question come at me so thick and fast that I can barely grab one here and there and figure out what I'm supposed to understand and what I'm really supposed to answer. The other guys have also gotten pale and opened their eyes as wide as their boots; even smartass Parrot's keeping his mouth shut to avoid catching the reporter's eyes, which are popping out of his face in pure meanness. I say, Yes, Captain. The Captain says, Don't address me, but the journalist. I answer, Yessir, Mr. Journalist, everything's fine, we're getting enough to eat and we don't have any complaints. The others nod their heads and mouth their agreement to back up their old buddy who's on the spot. I'm thinking what great guys they are and how they stand by you. By now, that mutt must be making off with some food while everybody's concentrating on our touchy situation. The Captain bites his mustache and puts his hands on his pot, which has started shaking like a great big bowl of Jello. We whisper among ourselves that the Captain's getting sore, and we move back a little, just in case. The reporter glances as cool as ever over at the Captain and says, Please repeat my question to the soldier, because it looks like here in the army everything's done according to the chain of command. The Captain swallows to keep from swearing and smiles at me with his yellow teeth showing, which look like they're ready to grind up our souls, and we're shitting in our pants. He says, Please tell him what our food's like. Well, no harm in telling anybody that: in the morning we get . . . the goofy dog's behind the Captain now and it's peeing right on his pack. The reporter says he's already heard all about the cooked corn, but what else? Speak right up, because the Captain says you may, he says, forcing a phony smile for manners and political reasons. The others are sweating in their places, thanking God the sly bastard hasn't tangled with them. Parrot looks like he's no longer among the living; he's holding his breath so even his stomach won't move. Well, once we got some nice packages from some . . . The Captain steps backward, pretending to scratch his ear, and signals to me from behind the reporter's back not to even mention the business about the gringos who came last week with their packages and their smiles. The Captain's jelly-belly's about ready to bust now. I notice that the dog's now sticking his muzzle in the Captain's pack; he must have gotten hold of something worth while, cuz he's holding the pack with his forepaws and pulling like mad. The reporter puts on a fake expression of surprise, because he realizes my predicament and prefers that I don't go on because he understands perfectly. He says, If the Captain does not object, I'd like to ask another soldier a question, you, the short one standing behind everybody else. And Parrot the wise bastard says, Who, me, sir? Yes, precisely, you, my dear young recruit. I'm thinking, Now you've had it, Parrot; let's see you bullshit your way out of this one so the Captain won't kick your ass afterwards. The reporter says something, and I see the dog has pulled a pair of dirty shorts out of the Captain's pack and is having a great hell of a time ripping it up with his teeth and claws. Parrot answers that up till now he hasn't even seen a guerrilla dead or wounded, he hasn't even seen a guerrilla prisoner. The Captain's jelly-belly's splitting his pants, the mutt's playing around with his shorts, and I'm wondering what the hell did we do to deserve all this.

I jump when the Captain's voice thunders in my ear and a spray of spit hits my face. I keep saying, Yessir, I understand, sir, and I'm thinking to myself, Holy shit. The Captain steps over in front of Parrot and yells his dire warning right in his face: "Listen, you bastards, from now on nobody's sneaking out of here at night and whoring around. We're here to do a job, not to show people how degenerate we are. Get it?" Parrot says, Naturally, sir, I feel I understand perfectly. The Captain says, Cut out that damn smartass crap; who the hell do you think you are? The Parrot says, Yessir. The Captain, hitching up his lovely stomach with an energetic jerk on his belt, repeats his warning again because, he says, we're moving out now to take up our positions, and we have to keep our eyes peeled and get our minds off women. "I repeat, off women!" he barks, "and dammit I mean to be obeyed." We all shout, Understood, sir, in

59

unison, and Parrot cracks under his breath, Everybody's got a right to his own illusions.

We fall out and go to our bunks. Parrot says he's got it right up to his neck, fed up with hanging around here without ever seeing a guerrilla or anything like one, and on top of it all they won't even give you any time off to take out a little piece ready for some loving. I tell him I know it's inhuman, but orders are orders. He cuts me off and says he found out a couple nice little whores just got into town but they're for officers only. I advise him, Pipe down if you don't want the Sarge to kick your ass. Parrot leers over at me with those dirty little eyes sparkling, and I can see the wheels turning. He puts one hand on my shoulder and starts rubbing his chin with the other; that's a sign he's working out something big. Now he's coming to the point: he's got the word about something the guys'll be real glad to hear. Across the street from the officers' whorehouse there's a nice little piece serving the troops; she lives by herself, and the frisky way she has of swinging her ass has earned her the nickname "Filly." Filly, old buddy! Get it? Parrot sighs deeply and looks out to where the jungle rises up, dark and spooky. He keeps saying "Filly, Filly," as if it were the name of some sweet-smelling flower. "What do you say?" he says, and I tell him, Don't be such a damn fool; if the Sergeant comes by and doesn't find us here it'll be hell to pay. So he says he'll sneak out by himself if only I promise to keep my mouth shut and be a buddy and help him. I ask him if he has enough money for the thing. He has, he says, since he's been saving up just for this one last bust. One last fling,

60

he says, and winks and gives me his big, shit-eating grin. I tell him, I envy you, but be real careful. He says he knows what he's doing, but just the name of that little whore's got him so roped he can't resist the temptation; and anyhow, as the Captain would say, "Fuck 'em all."

The Captain's yelling, Where the hell'd all the goddam soldiers go? We're running all over hell shooting up the jungle and I'm thinking about Parrot, who this time's really up shit's creek. The Sergeant keeps running around with his revolver in his hand. "It might be just a trick to get us to leave the camp," says the Captain. I fire toward where the shots came from in the jungle. But the shots we heard weren't repeated. I'm thinking it's just something somebody thought up to get us off our ass, but maybe they're just sitting tight waiting for one of us to stand up or stick up his head. When you're waiting for what may never come, time's like a slow river that stands still just before rounding the bend so it won't cross your sight. The Captain's worried over the troops under his command and asks if anyone's hit or maybe even dead. I look into the dark forest and think of Parrot. The Sergeant asks, Did you hear me? I heard you, Sarge, but I'm watching to see if anyone's coming out there. He asks again, Did Parrot take off cuz he's chickenshit? Hell no, Sarge, I tell him, he just got lost in the shuffle after the attack, and I didn't notice where he went. The Sarge asks me, Yeah, but was the shuffle during the shooting? I blurt out "Yeah," but the word almost gets stuck in my throat. The Captain's spotted something, a little spot lighter than the surround-

61

ing shade, and tells us, Be on your guard. The Captain crouches down behind a wall and says to me, Get your ass down, too. The Sergeant says, We'll surprise him and take him alive and kicking. I'm laughing to myself, because I can see the way the spot's walking; I'd recognize him blindfolded. The Captain's got the shakes from waiting, and he whispers, "Better take him alive so he'll talk." I'm thinking this guy's not even going to want to give his name, and it's all I can do to keep from laughing right in the Captain's face and spoil his fun. The Sergeant, his voice piping with emotion and his heart pounding in his chest, says, Hold it right there, you bastard; put up your hands and don't try to signal anybody behind you. Everybody's aiming at him. The Captain gives him clipped instructions in his crisp tone, Come forward with your hands up and turn around. Parrot says, What's wrong, Cap, for God's sake don't shoot. The Captain says, Christ, it can't be! The Sergeant says, Tenshun, you little bastard! He stands at attention while I go over and try to explain what happened to the Captain and the Sergeant, who are still aiming at him from their hiding places. Parrot's shaking, and his eyes, in the twilight, have lost that sly glint they had before leaving for his adventure with Filly. And the Sergeant says, Yeah, it's the Parrot all right. And I whisper to Parrot, Better get your fly zipped up right away. "Thanks, buddy," he mumbles weakly. "It's Parrot, Sarge," I say in a loud voice to drown out Parrot's remark; he's been fooling around with that whore while our lives have been hanging in the balance. The Captain goes over to him, his lungs heaving; I want an explanation, soldier.

62

Parrot's at a loss for words and looks over at me for help. I'm thinking that, as far as I can see, this is probably Parrot's last fling. The Sergeant's got a contented grin spread all over his face and says, Captain, this man's the bravest guy in my whole squad. The Captain's still not convinced and asks more questions with a spark of doubt in his eyes. Parrot explains, as soon as I heard the first shot and the bullet grazed my ear, Captain, I grabbed my rifle and plunged into the bush to catch the bandits. The Captain says he thinks this is an act of boldness worthy of imitation. "That damn Parrot, I don't know how he does it; no matter where he is, just toss him in the air and he always lands feet first," I'm thinking, glad to have him as a friend.

The sun spreads its rays of light o'er mount and vale,
waking bird and beast and man:

The man has come to the riverbank. He stands behind
some tall bushes. The day begins as always in the jungle,
with the birds taking flight and filling every place with
their song, with a new voice different from the buzzing
of its insects, the roar of its beasts, and the crawl of
its lizards and snakes. "No one around," the man says
to himself, looking about in all directions, and he begins
to undress.

Chaco looks down at him from the hill and smiles.
Then he notices a young girl on the opposite shore who
has also begun to undress quickly. He wants to warn
his companion, but checks himself for fear of startling
the girl.

"The water's cold," the girl says to herself as she
wades out until the water touches her waist. She squeals

softly at the shock of dipping her breasts into the cold water.

The man stands up and looks cautiously across the river. He is still holding one of the boots he has just taken off. He watches the girl laughing to herself as she splashes around in the water. His hand lets go of the boot, which falls soundlessly on the grass. The girl laughs and sings a song that is a strange new melody to his ears.

If my sight deceives me not, I thought to see 'twixt branch and branch a nymph to yonder font arrive:

Chaco leaned against a tree to watch better. "Javier's a good boy," he said to himself, "but let's see what he does now." The sun's rays began to heat the place rapidly, as is possible only in the jungle; there, heat comes with the dawn, in the twinkling of an eye, almost at once.

Javier lay down in the grass and brushed aside some branches blocking his view of the bathing girl. Her body was bronze beneath the sun. Javier looked around for Chaco, but could not spot him. "He must be off somewhere," he said to himself. The girl was swimming now. A hummingbird hovered a moment before Javier, painting a tiny rainbow in the air. In the background, the girl stood up on the beach. Perceiving a human presence, the hummingbird whisked away with the speed of light. The girl danced a few steps in the sand. Her nakedness studied thus in the sunlight heightened her beauty. "She's more than pretty," thought Javier. Her long black hair clothed, disclosed, screened, defined, disclosed again, her shining body. Suddenly she had an odd feeling that someone was observing her. She stopped. She glanced down both banks of the river. Everything seemed quiet; everything seemed to say that the breeze blew as before, that nothing new or strange appeared in the setting. But the uneasiness, the suspicion, had lodged in her mind and would not leave her. "Somebody must be near," she said to herself with increasing anxiety.

Chaco starts sweating and wishes Javier would get the thing over with once and for all. "He'll just stay put until she's dressed and goes away; he won't pull anything," he tells himself. He moves into the shade. "He's a wonderful kid," he thinks, feeling pride in Javier's behavior, unthinkable in the friends he used to run around with in his home town. He sits down and enjoys the refreshing peacefulness of the shade. "Javier's my best comrade; he's incapable of doing anything to disgrace the cause."

For you I loved the hush of shady wood, the distance and disdain of lonely mount:

The young man thought the girl was looking at him. He shuddered in embarrassment. But she could not be seeing him, because she continued to search his side of the river and then turned to examine her side. "She's beautiful," Javier said to himself, overcome by an undefinable something, by a presence in his soul subtler than the flight of the hummingbird. "She's the most beautiful girl I've ever seen in my life," he thought.

Chaco could not see the girl from where he was. But Javier was still in sight, and he saw him raise himself up a little, cup his hands around his mouth, and say something to the girl, who now appeared in his field of vision and walked hurriedly to where she had left her clothes. Chaco smiled.

And in this very vale where now I grow weary and sad, I rested happy and content. The good, oh 'tis so shallow, frail, and fleeting.

Javier cupped his hands around his mouth and said, "Good-by." He lowered himself again and saw her no longer, repeating the words louder and louder: "Good-by, good-by." He had to force himself not to raise his head to catch another glimpse of her; he lay in the grass, closed his eyes, and savored the sad aftertaste left by those images of possible ventures never lived. It was one of those stirrings, one of those far-off specks, that lead us to fancy chains of events that never come to be.

Chaco watched the girl dress, and saw her throw about her shoulders the only dress she owned; she pulled it down and tied up her loose hair, and, looking around nervously, started up the footpath until she became lost in the vegetation.

The girl looked around once again and ducked into the grove. "There was someone there all the time," she said to herself, trying to remember the words she thought she heard at the river. It could not have been something she had imagined. Her heart was pounding. "I won't say anything about it to Father," she thought.

Those bright eyes, where are they now, that bore my soul wheresoever they turned:

'Let's go,' said Chaco solemnly, pretending he had not seen.

Javier finished putting on his boots and stood up. 'Decided not to take a bath,' he said.

'There's not time,' said Chaco.

Javier picked up his rifle and began to walk.

'Something wrong?' Chaco asked him.

"And where now the hand so fine and fair?" Javier kept walking, not hearing his comrade.

'You look strange, old man.'

Javier stopped and looked at Chaco. His eyes, as green and shining as those of a lynx, beamed in friendship. "Where the soft breast now?"

'Man?'

Chaco winked and nodded toward the river. 'It's all over, in the past now. It can't hold us back; get it, man?'

Javier gave him his hand.

'We're going to build,' Chaco said after a while.

'In what we're going to build, nothing will remain of the past nor of ourselves,' he said; 'do you understand, man? Nor of ourselves either!'

Javier repeated, to Chaco's surprise, the verses from the poet, which were already on his lips:

'*All this, alas for me, is now locked away in cold, hard, barren earth.*'

The two friends arrived in camp.

The first thing that I noticed, that we all noticed, was his eyes: sincere, like a kid's. He came into the patio saluting everybody, with his hand making it all the way to his forehead. The Captain came out to meet him with a great, big, friendly smile and shook his hand. We all thought a hell of a lot of that Lieutenant. The pot-bellied ol' Captain was careful not to let loose with one of his broadsides of heavy-caliber words, and it looked like his tongue was so disappointed it was about ready to walk out on strike.

The Lieutenant comes in and says the men in the other squad have to mobilize and make a quick recon of a ravine, because the peasants have reported they've seen suspicious people in there. I wish I could go with the Lieutenant, but it's just a wish. You can see he's a man who knows how to command and also how to act to get his men to imitate him. As if he guessed what I'm thinking, he looks at me and asks if I'd like to be going along. I'd really like to go, Lieutenant; I'd like to go on a daring mission in the service of my Country. He smiles. I guess cuz I talked gung-ho like a kid. Parrot's beak's open, but he's quiet; this guy's not the type Parrot mouths off around. But afterwards he starts bullshitting me and says the reason he doesn't want to go's because Filly's got a real deep-down need for him. The Lieutenant says, Of course the rest of you are going, but after we move out first. His voice has that strong-gentle quality of a real leader.

The patrol sets out with the Lieutenant at its head. The Captain sends him off with a wave of his hand; his tongue is already feeling the effects of its liberation. The Sergeant says, We'd better get ready, too, cuz we'll be pulling out an hour from now. "That guy's a pretty damn good lieutenant," says the Captain, rightly praising the Lieutenant, who in the two days he's been with us, has proven he's got what it takes. Even Parrot approves of him, except that now the only thing that matters for Parrot is the object of his rapture, the local Filly with the frisky ass. "Shit, I'd follow him to hell and back," says the Sergeant. I guess that about sums up what we all feel because . . . Okay everybody hurry up and get under cover, cuz shooting's been heard up ahead. No one's going to knock off our Looey. We're firing in the air to make some noise to scare off the bandits who ambushed the Lieutenant's patrol. You can't move fast on stones with water running over them, cuz they're as slippery as bars of soap. Keep running and shooting.

And yelling. The Sarge's face is red and wet with sweat like a strangled bullfrog, shouting and shooting. The stones are regrouping against our advance. Everybody hollering, Get those motherfucking bandits. War is supposed to follow some law, but hell, this isn't anything like any law where two men have the guts to fight it out man to man. This is dying without knowing, without helping anybody, just cuz some bastard's hiding behind something and shooting; the guy doesn't even know where the hell he's shooting, he just knows he's shooting, and you don't even hear it cuz you're already dead. And you never even see an enemy. Shit, dying here means all of a sudden getting a hole in you, and you don't even see anybody, and you don't hear the goddam bullet that comes and takes away your life.

Parrot's puffing like a locomotive and shooting up the whole ravine. Down at the bottom, the Looey's patrol is pinned down, not moving an inch. They're hugging the ground, wishing they could dig a hole with their breath.

And then silence. Nobody's firing, and the Sergeant's running all over hell, his eagle eye taking everything in. Okay, that's it, knock it off. The bandits have disappeared without a trace, as if the earth had swallowed them up. That's the way they fight. That's why our mouth feels so empty; we don't get our teeth into anything but air—and air that tastes like death.

Parrot's telling the soldiers at the bottom of the gully to come on up cuz there's no more danger. But they can't yet, cuz they're making a stretcher to get someone's body out who got shot up. Parrot asks who was it that got it. And the voice repeats again and again from the bottom of the gorge like a garbled echo or a whirl of sorrow and disbelief: It's the Looey, it's the Looey. . . .

The man watches his crouched companion. He whistles, and the sound floats over the tangled mass like an unseen bird. The man looks back at his companion. They both listen.

'No answer,' says the man; but then they hear an identical whistle, an imitation of the cry of a bird, drawn out by the distance.

His companion stands up and begins to walk; his eyes dart cautiously into every corner of underbrush where he hears the slightest noise. "Chaco hears things that I'll never hear," the man thinks as he walks with his gun in his hands, safety off.

They descend the hill and come to the river. The man pauses a moment, as he always does when he comes to this part of the river.

'Let's move,' whispers Chaco.

The song of a rare bird is heard from the left. Chaco

answers. The man turns his eyes away from the river. He begins to cross the ford. Around his body, the lead-colored glass of the river spreads out in rings that lose themselves in the dense darkness of the distant surface. Chaco wades on ahead. The water reaches his waist.

"She was bathing right here," Javier says to himself. The current is not strong; it looks more like a large pool.

'The water's warm at this hour,' whispers Chaco.

'Yeah, I know,' replies Javier.

"The water was up to her waist," he thinks.

Chaco has reached the other bank and is waiting. He starts out again when Javier catches up. Before climbing the footpath, Chaco hisses three times, like the song of a water snake. They answer from the other side.

'Fine,' says Chaco.

Chaco's footsteps are soundless. His comrades wanted to nickname him "the Cat," but he didn't like the idea. "That can mean other things, too," he snapped harshly. Nobody ever used the nickname again.

Javier pauses a moment to catch a last glimpse of the quiet water at the bottom of the path, now barely suggested by its glow.

His wet trousers begin to bother him as he walks. Javier thinks about the girl at the river again. "She must live around here," he says to himself. He feels sure he'll never see her again, and the thought leaves an unpleasant trace in his mind. But he shouldn't be thinking about anything right now. He recalls the Party's battle song, and his spirits gradually pick up as he repeats it to himself.

The song was over by the time they got to the top

of the hill. They have to walk a little farther before seeing the farmhouse, among the trees, standing out a little darker than the surrounding foliage, like a gray bug lodged in a cluster of dark twigs.

'Let's wait for the signal now,' says Chaco, and he hides behind a chestnut tree. Javier does the same. From where he stands, he can just make out the sound of the song his companion is humming. Chaco can hum a song and at the same time listen perfectly to the jungle. "My mother taught me," he answers whenever his comrades show their surprise.

'Everything's okay,' Chaco said, and he bounces up like a cat and begins walking, all in the same motion as if running on electric motors.

The two men take up their positions in the sparse banana orchard. The dog from the house has begun to bark. Chaco has halted.

'Let's circle the house first,' says Chaco.

'Okay,' says Javier, and starts off.

Their two bodies separate and move off in different directions. They dart from tree to tree, jerky, like a silent movie. They meet again where they started. The dog has not quit barking.

'Everything's fine,' says Chaco, 'let's go.'

Javier walks behind Chaco. As the men draw closer, the dog's bark becomes a mournful howl. They arrive at the low wall of pressed earth that surrounds the house. From there they watch the dog, which is now scratching at the door and whimpering in fear. The hens are also in an uproar.

'They're talking inside the house. We better make it snappy,' says Chaco.

The two men hurdle the wall and head for the chicken coop. The door of the farmhouse opens and the dog shoots in like a bullet. Javier hides behind the door. Someone runs out brandishing a machete, trips over the animal, and stumbles. Javier reaches out his arm and grabs a wrist, and with his other hand covers a mouth. Then Javier realizes, for his skin has touched unexpected smoothness, that the girl from the river is in his arms, trembling with fear.

The Captain says, You men today have carried out a memorable feat; we're thinking, Come off it. Then he says, You really gave it to the bastards, and we breathe a sigh of relief. The Sergeant says, With the Captain's permission, and the Captain, Go right ahead. So he starts his speech all choked up, I'd like to recall to your mind the memory of the Lieutenant who came to lead the attack on the ravine. Even Parrot's sniffling a little. The Captain breaks in on the Sergeant's speech, Now we got another reason for kicking the shit outta those hairy red bastards; it could have been any one of us; I mean we could have been killed instead of the Lieutenant. Death can come faster than thunderless lightning, the Captain finishes up. We're pretty broken up and feel real bad about the Looey. Even Parrot; he's usually screwing around all the time, but he's so quiet now you wouldn't think he's the old Parrot. The Captain says today's our last day in town cuz tomorrow's our next attack against the guerrillas. We'll make up an honor guard over the Lieutenant's body until they come to pick him up, and then we'll have a pass until eleven tonight. Parrot's starting to feel like his old self; Damn, he says, what a piece of luck! He's thinking about Filly. I'm thinking about her, too, wondering what she's like, cuz I haven't met her yet. From what Parrot's told me, I picture her as a big hunk of pleasure that's all his.

Am I on the make for her now? Of course not. I just know that glow Parrot gets when he talks about her. I just want a woman; any woman will do, not necessarily Filly. She's where Parrot goes to cool off his hot pants. That's all I'm after when I start feeling lonely, just any piece of ass. If someone else comes along before Filly, I won't give her a second thought.

The Captain said, Fall out. We're all standing around talking in little groups, making plans for tonight. I light a cigarette. Parrot says thanks and takes a drag, and we keep passing it back and forth. Then he looks at me and says, You know, you're not looking your old self lately, but if all goes well, I'll line up a little get-together tonight at Filly's. Seems she's got this little cousin of hers that's just what the doctor ordered. I tell him, Thanks for counting me in, and laugh. So I'm finally going to meet that Filly I've been hearing so much about.

We slap each other on the back and puff away like in the good old days, as if we didn't have to move out against the guerrillas again. I tell him, Shit, I wish tonight was here already, c'mon time, get moving! Don't be an asshole, Parrot says, Time can't hear you. I tell

80

him, Hell, it's moving, isn't it? Parrot thinks that's a great joke, but the Sergeant thinks we shitheads better get off our ass and get cleaned up, cuz we have to stand guard until they come from the city to take the body away. Again that damn sickening thought of death comes in to mess up our bright, happy little world. The Sergeant says, Okay, shine your boots and straighten up your uniforms. Parrot says if I cover for him he'll shoot over to Filly's to be sure the thing's on for tonight. Sure, old buddy, go on, take off. The Sergeant says these guys we're getting today are a bunch of degenerate morons, as he scratches his head and beams at me with pride.

The Captain beams at us with pride and says we acted with valor, and the General also beams at us with pride and says that is just what he expected from us. And we start carrying the coffin to the plane that's waiting on the airstrip. You weigh more when you're dead, cracks Parrot, sweat dripping off his face. Another soldier adds, Maybe it's because you're stiff as a slab of ice, and when you're dead you're weighted down with the sadness of the people who see you. I'm thinking we shouldn't be talking like that. The plane's sitting in the middle of the runway, and the runway's long enough to wear you out. Our clothes are getting soaked with sweat. Sometimes I think that a guy shouldn't die so far away from home, but of course the Looey didn't die, he was killed, and that's different; actually that's an entirely different matter. An officer says, Set it down here first. Okay, we say. He says, I'm a lieutenant, see the bar? Okay, Lieutenant. This guy's about as different from the dead Lieutenant as you can imagine: a skinny runt with a face like a horse's, only bigger lips, and with snooty eyes. He says, Straighten it out like this; okay, now lift; you'd think you dumb fools'd figure it out for yourself; do you think I'm talking Chinese? The coffin seems heavier, now that we're tired. The Lieutenant says, With an army full of guys like you, the guerrillas'll be in La Paz next week. At last the coffin's in place. Death's a witch's curse pointing at you with a crooked finger. They would have to pick this prick of a lieutenant. His back is to us, and Parrot looks at him and gives him the up-yours sign. We all laugh. And Parrot says, So I went like this to that little shit of a lieutenant, and Filly starts laughing like hell. The tips of her tits are bouncing around, sending out a nice invitation. But I'm looking at the cousin; she didn't laugh, and she's fatter than Filly and not as nice. I'm thinking, Well, what the hell are you going to do, that's just my luck. The Parrot's got a long line of shit to give Filly, so he winks at me, meaning I should get the cousin out of the room. Fatso says great, she'd like "real much" to go for a little walk with me. I grab her shoulder and put my arm around her and start getting right down to it. Filly's already hugging Parrot; you can see she's a hot number and knows what she's doing—as she should, being in her profession.

But is Filly any better than most women? No. She's a whore who knows how to hustle, but her affections don't last. She just gives what you pay for. Real love is different, it's loving a woman forever. It's letting her own your soul. It's not being afraid she'll forget you, or not having to hide what you really are. One thing's for sure: Filly's nicer than that tub of a cousin who's playing hard to get. But Filly isn't the nicest woman I can think of. Why the hell do I think she's so special?

From the house, you keep hearing Filly's giggling and Parrot's fooling. Fatso sits under a big tree in the garden where there's shade and you can hear the birds chirping. She keeps talking about Cochabamba because she went there once and I'm from around there. She says it's such a real nice place . . . and I shut her mouth with a kiss. She wants to put up a fight over it, but my pants have been getting hotter and hotter ever since they brought us to this damn place, and I couldn't let go of her waist if I wanted to. So I start at the beginning and put my hand on what Filly would have offered with a lot less fuss.

'I've come to you,' says the man.

She lowers her eyes and bites her lips. At night she heard the footsteps of some men who paused briefly by the house and went on.

'They're back!' the old man cries, running over to his daughter's hammock to be ready to protect her. The dog growls and scratches at the door; it creaks open, sounding like a dying bird. Laura clings to the old man.

'They won't come in, Father,' she whispers in his ear.

'Just to be with you,' says the man as he takes her face in his hands and lifts it to meet his own.

Your face is the face I saw at the river. Your eyes are those I still bear within; they gaze at me and say that you, too, are where I live, in the air I breathe.

'They won't come in,' the girl repeats.

The dog inside the house starts howling. The men move on. Now she *knows* he is one of them. The half-light still reveals no objects. Outside, the fog begins to creep down from the mountains, softly.

The men halt in front of the house. They can barely make it out through the mist. "The fog will cover everything," the men think. They continue on their way, their hands firmly grasping their guns.

'It's dawning,' the old man says.

'But the fog keeps coming down,' says Laura, peering out through a small open window among the palm leaves.

I touch your hand, I open your resisting fingers. The softness of your skin awakens my desire. Your eyes hold me in their steady gaze. Your fingers begin to yield, the slowness of their surrender making my joy the fuller. Our fingers are now woven together; you close your eyes, then open them, and your cheeks flush, on fire.

Out beyond the fog, there are hints the day is beginning. The old man does not want to leave the hammock. The dog trembles and growls in the corner.

'I came by here at dawn,' says the man.

"I heard you come," the girl thinks. "They were your footsteps. I even think I heard your breath. Your breath came to me on the breeze at the river, and now it has come to me in the mist."

'Don't go out there, Laura,' says the old man.

'I have to go down to the river for water,' says Laura, and she leaves.

"She'll never come back," the old man thinks. "Her mother went to the river like that, and she never came back. . . . I'll be left all alone." The old man sits down in his hammock. The dog has calmed down, and curls up at his master's feet.

'Poor old Blackie; you're just like me,' the old man says.

The sun has broken up the fog. The sticky heat oils the skin and makes it shine.

The men stand on the edge of the ravine, which falls off and loses itself in a thicket. They begin picking strategic locations. Each selects a precise spot and moves with the skill of a man who knows his job. The Chief needs to give only a few orders; he usually just nods to the questions the others ask. The fog in the ravine still manages to withstand the sun's effects. After a few minutes, nobody moves; everything's set. Now hardly any fog remains at the bottom of the ravine. The murmur of the water is more audible now. The men wait patiently, not speaking to one another, their eyes fixed on the floor of the gully.

Your breath mingles with mine, shaping a single breath that lives from what we give. Your hands are now gentle doves alighting upon my shoulders, opening wide your realm to me. Your breath is so close now I draw away slightly for fear of hurting your soft, pure skin.

The Chief takes his cap off and lays it aside. His neck is sweating profusely. Chaco is lounging comfortably against a tree.

'We came by very early.'

'I knew it was you,' says the girl.

The girl fills the water jug with a gourd. The mist has almost gone; only the river still holds a trace. She leaves the jug on the sand and looks at the opposite bank. "He came by in the dawn," she says to herself, and touches her wrist, where she still feels the fingers of the man who held it that night they came to take the chickens. "He's a bandit; he kills people. Just this morning he went off to kill," she tells herself, trying to remove the hand and the breath that again stroke her neck.

'You've come back,' says the old man happily; his smile reveals his toothless gums.

'Yes, Father. Everything's fine.'

The old man gets up from the hammock and goes over to the door. The house is completely surrounded by banana trees. After a few steps, the old man suddenly halts in alarm.

'I hear shots,' he says with a look of fear.

'Oh no,' the girl cries, looking at the old man and reaching out toward him. "God, please don't let him get killed," she thinks.

The sun has reached its zenith. Laura and the old man eat, sitting on the floor facing each other, in silence. The dog lies between them and waits for them to throw him some food.

'Laura, I've come because I love you,' says the man.

I fondle your hair. Your hair, black as the very sanctum of life. Life springs from the shadow of your eyes, from your hair, and fills the world, my world.

The two look up, through the bower, at the moon, laced with dark patchwork. The girl sighs, and the man takes her into his arms again.

'The shooting has stopped,' the old man announces.

'That's them!' says Chaco, bouncing up and grabbing his gun.

Everyone stares at him. They know that there are soldiers behind the bend in the ravine, invisible to them but present to Chaco's ears.

88

The men cock their weapons and hold their breath. The Chief picks up his cap and puts it on leisurely. A green spot appears at the bottom of the ravine. It moves cautiously and holds up beside an immense rock. It signals, and another spot comes out from behind, and another. . . . Chaco is counting, his voice hissing through his teeth.

'That's the last of them. Let them get up higher,' says the Chief.

'They'll be back. They'll be coming back,' worries the old man.

'We're bringing a casualty, Grandpa,' says the man standing in the door.

Laura stands motionless in a corner of the room.

'We have nothing to offer you. We can't help you,' replies her father.

'We want some boiling water to take care of him,' says the man, and adds, 'We'll pay.'

The old man scratches his head and glances into the corner where Laura is hiding.

'I'll get some for you,' she says, and gets busy.

The man watches her emerge from the shadows almost without surprise. Laura passes by him and goes outside.

'Thanks,' says the man, and follows her out.

Your lips part. As yet they have known no kiss, but now they desire it. They would flee when I bring my mouth near, but they cannot; desire holds them there. Your lips are waiting. When at last I touch them with my own, they open for my life to surge into the waiting sanctum of your soul.

'Does it hurt, Chaco?' Javier asks the wounded man.

'This one's mine,' says Chaco, and he carefully lines him up in the sights of his automatic. Javier can see the young officer's weary expression; he can see the beads of sweat forming on his face while he pauses to catch his breath. The officer raises his hand to his forehead to wipe off the sweat. He suspects nothing. He's completely preoccupied with his physical fatigue. There's a faint crack, and Javier blinks as he sees the officer's face erased from the landscape. It just disappeared, as if a screen painted with rocks and plants had covered it up. Javier turns his head away and catches the unintended grin of pleasure on Chaco's face. More than anything in the world, he would like to drive away the echo of that shot which blotted out the officer forever, but now he, too, is shooting and not thinking about anything any more, just about erasing, himself erasing, the picture of the sweaty officer and all the officers in the world.

'You are my purity, Laura,' says Javier. 'Everything else is death, oblivion, do you understand?'

The moon comes to a star-filled clearing in the foliage. Now you can see all of it. They, Javier and Laura, say it is beautiful; it is beautiful like that, in its course, free of the dark tangle that sometimes hides it.

'He's my friend,' he says, pointing to the wounded man.

Laura looks at him and says nothing. She blows on the coals to coax up a flame.

'My name's Javier,' says the man.

'Mine's Laura.'

And now our joy is full; it lives again, thrilling, throbbing in us, whimsically, Laura, you and I. We hold each other close like this; we shut our eyes to see each other.

Chaco groans in pain. His whole body is shaken in convulsions. The fire dances over the coals.

'The water will boil soon,' says Laura and looks at the wounded man. 'Poor man,' she adds.

Javier looks at her and reaches out his hand to touch her arm. She draws back a little, but then relaxes.

'I'll come back one of these nights, whenever I can get away,' Javier tells her.

'The soldiers will come,' says the old man inside the house.

Night begins in the jungle. At first, it casts its shadow in the hollow of the tree trunks, then it sends its fingers to the tangled foliage. Then, like a silent cat, it sets its paws on the ground and lies down to cover everything.

'We'll have to take off as soon as I get the bullet out and bind up the wound,' says one of the men.

Laura looks at Javier. The two are standing facing one another, gazing into each other's eyes; their hands are hidden in the shadows.

'I'll come back,' Javier repeats.

Your skin shies, then draws near again. My body hungrily folds it in; seizes, releases. And now it is your skin seizing my own, keeping it, giving of its smoothness.

The old man begins to snore. The girl gets up from her hammock. She goes toward the door and opens it with the greatest caution, placing her fingers on the doorpost. The door creaks softly. The old man's snoring breaks off.

Laura waits. He tosses heavily in the hammock and begins to snore again. Laura squeezes through the narrow opening. The dog comes over to her, wagging his tail.

'Be quiet, Blackie,' the girl says.

She looks toward the nearest trees. She raises her eyes to the sky. The maze of vegetation barely lets her see the moon. She starts. Someone's hand has taken her wrist. The dog continues to wag his tail.

'I've come back,' says the man.

Parrot says, I've had it with this fucking life, and I ask him, What the hell do you want, shithead; this is how we're supposed to be serving our Country. Parrot says, I'd like to put one question to you, if I may. Yes, you may. What the hell do you have to say now? C'mon, servant of our Country, answer me that. Parrot's laugh attracts the Sergeant's attention. The Sarge says, What are you two idiots cackling about like a couple of hens; now spread out and move your asses. Parrot walks on ahead and crouches down when he gets to the rocky place. It'd make you laugh to see him walking like that, all bent over. You dumb goof-off Parrot. I've noticed lately that Parrot hasn't been his old deep-down Parrot self, cuz he's always thinking of Filly. Filly's just a whore, but she sure as hell's gotten under his skin. I told him, Don't be an asshole; you'll be sorry if you get mixed up with that whore. But he said, Up yours, and you never can tell. I walked right in then. He was smoking a cigarette and leaning back in Filly's hammock and told me to take a good look at that woman over there and points to her. By now, my tongue's hanging out for her. And Filly puffs up her tits and looks over at me defiantly and says she doesn't like anybody pointing at her and who do we think she is. Parrot says, Excuse me, baby, and she answers, It's all right, and he says, Y'see that little Filly over there, well that's my baby you're looking at, and by damn she's going to be my wife. Filly smiles, flashes her empty gums, and I'm wondering what the hell kinda horseshit is Parrot giving me now. Parrot, do you realize what you're saying? I know you're a big nut and a bullshitter, but for God's sake, Parrot, do you know what you are doing? Of course I say this later, not in the room in front of Filly. Parrot's looking at me, and then he groans, and says, Why the hell didn't you tell me right then when I proposed to her? I explain. Parrot, you better cool off about that woman, get it? He says, Yeah, but you know there are cases where whores have made much better wives than those lily-white virgins that you have to pick up at their house if you want to take them out. *I've started to think about the possibility of me paying her a little visit myself. Does friendship mean anything to that type woman? Hell no. It has nothing to do with friendship. She just gets to you when she swings her fanny like a frisky little mare. It's not a question of love. It's just the devil tempting me to screw her.* Parrot jumps and dives into the middle of a bush when the bullets start blasting all around. The Sergeant says, Just our goddam luck, it's an ambush,

94

boys; get down, you bastards, and don't move. I'm down behind a rock praying to the Virgin of Copacabana to get me out of this. Parrot must be praying, too, right in the middle of that sticker bush, and cussing out the guerrillas and the army, and probably thinking of his Filly and telling her "Just wait up for me, Filly baby, cuz you know what our plans are. If I get out of this, we'll go up to La Paz." And then the local Filly opens her big eyes, and tells him she's going to make a great housewife; like when she sticks her tongue out at me in front of the hammock and shows me her gums without a trace of a good tooth, and then she starts wiggling her behind like something out of a Mexican movie; and Parrot's laughing and pinching her ass. How are you supposed to know what life's all about and what God's got lined up for you, when He's so stubborn about not letting you see the future? He probably even surprises Himself with what turns up in His creation. Because either He takes care of us like even a mangy old bird takes care of its baby birds, or else He doesn't care about us any more, so you can't know what will come of this; nobody can figure it out. The Sergeant yells at me, Dammit, man, are you deaf? Start shooting! So I'm shooting the place up. We hear the voices of the guerrillas coming from the bushes, C'mon, men, surrender, you're our friends; we don't have anything against you, just against your generals, who are agents of the imperialists, yankee ass-kissers. The Sergeant yells back, What the hell do you take us for? Just stand up where we can see you, and it'll be the last time you give that line to anybody. Parrot's probably shooting away like crazy, at anything that moves, for his Filly. For that little whore. Because if he gets out of this in one piece, he figures he can make his life with any woman he feels like; he doesn't give a damn if I approve of her or not. Filly runs up to the hammock and jumps on top of Parrot, and he says, Watch it, you'll get burnt with the cigarette. She did get burnt, but says she doesn't care and starts rubbing her arms and her tits up against Parrot's chest. Parrot says, Buddy, everything's going to turn out all right, because now you've seen the future missus and know what she's like. I go out sore and nail a rooster with a wad of spit, dozing in the shade of Filly's house with his hens. The Sarge says, The fucking bastards've got us this time; hold your fire, cuz you can't see 'em. The soldiers start swearing at the guerrillas, and the guerrillas make as if they don't hear. But they are not firing either. The Sergeant says, Hold it like this until the rear patrol gets up here. What the hell else can we do? Parrot must be in his hole, not moving a muscle so he'll get out alive and go back to his fair damsel. Someone opens up again from the bushes, and the Sergeant yells, You chickenshit bastards, come out and fight like men! Then the yell of a soldier, it seems more like a howl, it gets louder than the shooting; it gets in our ears like a big hand stuffed it in, and it starts buzzing around our heads like a hairy bug. The Sergeant says, They got the poor guy. I ask, Could it be Parrot, Sarge? He says, Hell, it can't be Parrot, cuz he's probably stretched out in his bush snoring away, lost to this world. I'm thinking that the old shithead always lands on his feet. But not in the Filly thing; that's for sure. Of course, you can never tell how she'll turn out. Actually, she's not that bad. She's really not that bad, because she's got a body like a tiger in heat. *She's not that bad? There I go again, thinking to myself what it'd be like to be Parrot when he's with Filly on their wedding night. Of course, she's an old hand at it. Naturally.* Filly looks at me and rubs her arm where the cigarette burned her. She asks, Aren't you glad about Parrot's choice? She laughs. I look at her with a mixture of anger and desire; Filly may be just a little hustler, but she sure is all female. The Sergeant asks me if I hear shots down by the mouth of the gully. I say, Not yet, Sarge, and he says, Shit, are you deaf? I answer, That's right, Sarge. Then he yells, Now we're going to beat the shit out of the hairy bastards. The afternoon passes quickly. You can already hear the rattle of a machine gun. Don't get up yet. I'm thanking God and the Virgin of Copacabana with all my heart. I say softly, Parrot; Parrot, you dumb shithead. The cry of the wounded soldier doesn't come to us any more. The Sergeant jumps up and says, Now we're going to give the bastards a lesson; okay, follow me. We get up and fire into the underbrush. We advance. I look all around and figure that Parrot's playing it cool, not budging from where he is until the rear patrol gets here. I go over to the bush he jumped in to stick the rifle butt up his ass. The evening is wrapped in a blanket of shadows. I come up to the bush and then, Let's go, shitface. Parrot. Bird-brain Parrot. C'mon, quit clowning around. Dammit, Parrot, that's enough screwing around, get up and . . . Parrot, I bet your face is all covered with mud in a puddle like that. It's all mud, Parrot. Look, Parrot buddy, all you have to do is get up, that's all. And tomorrow they'll give you a furlough, and you'll marry your Filly and spend the rest of your life with her, and you'll live happily ever after with no worries and have a bunch of kids, and she'll gradually forget about her old days in town. And that's it, Parrot. I swear. Look, Parrot, all you have to do is bounce out of there and wipe the mud off your face and slap the dust off your clothes; just wash your face and get the mud off, I mean that's all, and then make one of your wise remarks, and that's all. C'mon, Parrot, that's all there is to it, I swear. And now I'm hearing a little bird; he's not afraid, cuz the bullets aren't buzzing around any more. He starts singing so pretty, Parrot, right here in this bush growing up around your muddy, dusty boots. Y'know, Parrot, it looks like God Himself sent him to sing for you. Honest to God, Parrot, I really think so. Then the Sergeant makes the sign of the cross and says something that nobody understands, not even himself, and he puts his hand on my shoulder; and I feel Filly's hand and hear her crying, and watch the snot running down her face.

1.   Mario looks down at his dirty fingernails, edged with grime, and smiles. That's funny, knowing you can have dirty fingernails. It's wonderful, feeling your body can still get dirty, pick up dirt that must be cleaned off.

2.   Last night while I was on guard duty, I was thinking about my days in the seminary. So much hope, so much concern, and for nothing. No, that's not really true; it was a stage I had to go through to get where I am. I've managed to get to where I am now only by following out the paths I've followed. They were 'beautiful' days, full of unending search and unending disappointment. I wanted to find love and understanding where there was only cold formalism, the letter that kills. It's madness to try to find the warmth of a home where the fire of passion for the other, for our neighbor, is missing.

3.   Life in camp has its good points. Everyone's enthusiastic. Every day, we train in guerrilla warfare. We've had visits from some foreign intellectuals and newspapermen, all of leftist tendencies. They talk with us, and take our photographs, which will not be released until the fighting breaks out. The Chief has a tremendous talent for organizing. We think of his being here in our camp as a kind of guarantee. Every day, we have an hour discussion period, which we all take turns leading. The Chief contributes with his clear-cut, precise ideas, but he often leaves the solution of the problems to us. We study important books; we read novels and poetry. Chaco's getting me fired up on the idea of writing a novel on the guerrillas.

'You've already got your hero: me,' he kidded.
'Yeah,' I replied, 'I can write that your personality is like the Chaco: dry.'

4.   The Chief gave us a talk on the value of comradeship. I was thinking of Carlos as he spoke. "He's probably a priest already," I said to myself with a kind of nostalgia for the hours we spent together. Friendship is built on common concern, a spiritual concern, which discloses a common root in the two friends who love each other.

5.   There's no backing from the Party. It's not pushing anything in the cities. There seems to be a difference of opinion over procedures and leadership in regard to the guerrilla movement. Anyhow, we'll have some time; so we

keep practicing every day, getting ready for a long campaign, which may start in five months.

6.   We have to leave our base camp unexpectedly, and abandon our radio equipment, ammunition, etc. An army patrol made contact with one of our units guarding the approach through a ravine. The Chief told us that there was some evidence of a betrayal. This spoils our plans. Apparently they took one of our contacts in town for a cocaine peddler. They were suspicious of him because he was constantly going off into the jungle and spending money in large bills for big amounts of supplies.

7.   It seems the Chief isn't too well. He walks about the camp alone. We're all beginning to notice some sluggishness in his movements. We've been hounded from the time they wounded three men, and we're always on the move from one place to another. Up until today, the Chief hasn't shown any signs of being tired. Nobody dares bring it up to him. Everybody looks at me to do it, so I gather up my courage and go over to him.
'We've noticed you're not looking too well, comrade.'
'I'll get over it.'
I can't find any more words; I look up at the cloud-filled sky. 'A storm's threatening,' I say.
'No storm should turn us aside,' he says.
I lower my eyes and stare hard at him in admiration.
'I'm tired,' he says, looking away. 'The news from the cities isn't very encouraging. You should all know that we're going through a critical period.'
'We're ready for any sacrifice,' I say, feeling like a

kid rattling off his catechism lesson for the religion teacher.

'The Revolution is something we call pretty close,' says the Chief, 'and what's useless becomes a bother and a drag.'

The clouds become more heavily laden with dark gray patches. The breeze blowing in our faces now has a touch of dampness.

'You know, . . . I, too, think about what I'm doing and what I'm sacrificing for the Revolution,' says the Chief. 'I think about my children, of . . .'

Right at this instant we hear the sound of three or four shots from the rear guard. The Chief is up in a second, and we notice how he keeps on going without a stop, giving orders, as if this were the only thing in his life, as if he weren't sick.

8   While we're marching through the jungle, Chaco comes up and says to me, 'It's very possible that one of us will die in this struggle. If it's me, I want you to remember me, and tell somebody how I was, about how I fought for an ideal. . . .' He falls silent for a minute, his matter-of-fact mind grasping for words. He goes on, 'It's something that'll console me at the moment of my death. Don't you think that you don't quite die as long as somebody remembers you?'

'Yes, maybe. But you're not going to die here; you're in your own element,' I tell him.

He answers, 'Birds usually get killed in the air.'

I guess the source of these somber thoughts is the

weariness and the loneliness of feeling no one's backing us up.

9   We had a skirmish with the army; we laid an ambush for them. Chaco was wounded. Because we had no other way of helping him, we took him to a farmhouse. It turned out to be the girl's, the girl from the river. She did great. Her name's Laura. Laura. Her father was a bit afraid of us and of the army. Chaco was holding my hand and saying in his delirium: 'Don't forget about me; remember what I asked you to do.'
We left the house as soon as we fixed up Chaco. I promised Laura I'd be back.

10   The soldiers keep dogging us. There are a lot of problems. We're going around in circles, because we can't hole up any more in the heavy jungle (now that we lack trustworthy guides to keep us from suffering more losses), and we can't leave this more-open terrain either (because outside of this place, which has a pretty thick undergrowth, it's completely barren of vegetation, and it'd be a cinch for military aircraft against us). But despite the fatigue and a bit of discouragement (we all feel it, but it's no sign of any lack of revolutionary spirit), I find that here, up to a certain point, I'm more enthusiastic, because Laura's nearby. Tonight I'm taking off for her house. I know the soldiers are patrolling the place, but I must see her; already she's a part of my life. I think she's becoming more and more *the* part of my life. One central fact is usually true about human beings: even

though our motives be the loftiest ideals, we always feel the need to "pad" our life with a little ballast of reality. To put it better, we don't live any given moment of our idealistic existence in all its purity and intenseness; rather, we weave into it certain concerns, perhaps less lofty and less capable of attaining the pure ideal, but concerns which have the advantage over the higher ideals of being "handier," of having more of the taste and hue of life. This is why any man who makes his ideal into a castle in the clouds seems to us to be a dehumanized robot. Our relationship to persons of the opposite sex, and I don't mean only the sexual relationship, is one of these "paddings." But a conflict comes to the person when what is merely one of life's paddings is forced by the passion of love to become the very sap of life, and displaces the ideal which before was its nourishment. But what happens when the ideal dies?

11   The Chief spoke to us in candor. He said things weren't going too well, but neither was everything lost. It was certain that the government had intercepted important contacts in the cities. Therefore the government knows how many we are, where we are, and what our actual resources are. Finally he said that as a man of the Revolution he could not deceive us and that we should each of us be aware of the arduous and difficult struggle ahead. He quoted a couple of sayings from some revolutionary leaders, and wound up by pointing out that, because of the nature of our situation and in view of the fact that only the most steadfast have remained in the group, only those who really lived the Revolution, he

did not even consider the possibility of any desertion in the ranks.

After he finished, there was a long silence. Like we were all facing up to ourselves. And then, without anyone actually starting it, our battle song welled up in our throats. We embraced the Chief and moved out.

12   I'm thinking about the Revolution early this morning, as I curled up to stay warm. "Can it ever be stopped? Or is it simply the illusion of radical minds?" I ask myself. I cannot say yes to either question. Of course, we've lost several comrades. And they might manage to wipe us out. But we aren't the Revolution. We're just aware of it, that's all; we wish to embody it in our Country. The Revolution is a demand, an imperative, from man's very substance: if we wish to come to our full humanity and leave the night behind, this fearful mixture of man and beast, we must sow the Revolution.

13   This morning we came to a tiny village, almost lost on a jungle hillside. The dogs were already barking when we were quite a ways off, but they weren't too excited. When we came into the narrow outlying streets, the town was quiet. The dogs just snarled, but couldn't bring themselves to attack us. It was a miserable little town, without any church or market or even a plaza. We chose an empty area to assemble the villagers.

They were slow in assembling. Some of them were afraid, and they were hiding in the funniest places: under their flimsy beds, and one was in a corner covered with dirty laundry. We persuaded them to come out and told them there was no danger, because we weren't going to shoot and we just wanted some information and to talk a few things over.

While we were rounding the people up, the Chief stayed in the best "house" in town, the only one with whitewash. It belonged to the mayor, who somehow found out that we were nearby and took off for the jungle. His wife was there alone, a big woman with a long face and a hooked nose. When she saw the Chief's face, drawn with fatigue, she felt sorry for him, in spite of her hard look, and offered him a bed and even put on clean sheets. The Chief consented to "lie down" a minute, but he was so beat that he fell fast sleep.

'Poor man,' the woman said each time she looked at him.

'He's a bit sick,' I said.

'He's just tired,' a comrade corrected me.

'You should surrender. The soldiers were here five days ago; there are ten times more of them than you. They're better equipped. The Sergeant said they're going to pardon everyone that surrenders. I don't know,' said the woman.

'We're more than you think,' said a comrade, 'and we have the people's support.'

The people kept gathering in the area. They waited in silence. Some came with their children for extra protection. The day was barely beginning, over in the faraway hills. Some people came to the meeting with little oil lanterns. I couldn't figure out what they were for.

After we finally rounded up the whole town, including the local schoolmaster, who turned out to be friendly and well-spoken to the guys who asked him to come along, some of the comrades came over wanting to wake up the Chief. I was against it. I told them he was very tired and it'd be better to let him sleep for a while longer.

'The people are getting nervous,' said Chaco.

'But the Chief hasn't really slept in over a week,' I replied.

The woman backed me up. She said the townsmen were used to waiting. She told us how once a political representative from the region promised to visit them on a certain date to "ascertain the real issues on the grass-roots level" (when she said this, she blushed for fear of seeming too highfalutin), and the people waited in the schoolroom for the whole day. In the end the representative didn't even show up. 'Three months later he sent his apologies through an organizer of the Peasants' Union who went to La Paz,' the woman finished.

The sun was already warming up the countryside. I went out to take a look at the town. Everybody was standing. The men held their hats in their hands and turned them nervously by the brims; the women held their shawls despite the increasing heat. Some of the women were protectively clutching their children.

'The Chief will be here,' I said.

Jerónimo stood at my side. He said to the people: 'Before the Chief gets here to say a few words to you, we'd like to ask you a few things. . . . I'm going to ask you some questions, and please don't be afraid to tell me the truth. When was the army here?'

Jerónimo's voice sounded crisp and clear, but nobody moved or gave any sign of having understood the question. Jerónimo stated it again, this time more forcefully, accompanying it with an ominous fingering of his rifle.

A murmur of fear came from the crowd.

'They were here several days ago,' said the teacher at last, flashing a friendly smile.

'How many days ago?' asked Jerónimo without looking at him, staring into the crowd.

'Six days ago,' said a woman.

'Five,' a man corrected her, and then hunched his shoulders as if he wanted them to swallow his head.

'How many?' asked Jerónimo.

'A lot more than you,' said the teacher, obviously pleased, but I'm not sure if over the numerical superiority of the soldiers or over knowing so many details.

'There's more of us than are here. We never show our full hand,' said Jerónimo, now aiming his piercing stare at the teacher, who did not become unruffled.

The sun was pretty high and was singeing our scalps. Some of the women began to take their shawls off timidly.

'Did they say where they were going?' asked Jerónimo.

Nobody knew a thing.

'They left the way they came in,' said a woman.

'Where?' asked Jerónimo.

'Over there,' pointed the woman.

'To the south,' said the teacher, again pleased with his words.

'Did they say anything to you?'

'They offered to pay us for giving them information. None of us knew anything. We just heard rumors about you. They said, too, that when they defeat you and carry through the pacification of the countryside, they'll come back to build a bigger school,' said the teacher.

Jerónimo shot us a glance. He was tired, in spite of his great physical strength.

'They said that you'd steal everything from us,' ventured someone in the crowd whom we couldn't spot.

An old woman cast us a scornful glance and said, 'And that you don't believe in God or the Virgin.'

The few boys of the village looked at us indifferently. They were bunched together in one corner of the area.

'Can you tell us anything important that will help us?' I asked the crowd.

They didn't seem to hear me.

A child, how or from where I don't know, appeared before Jerónimo. He smiled up at him. Jerónimo hunkered down and took him in his arms.

'Do you go to school?' he asked, loud enough for all to hear.

'No, I help my papa out in his clearing,' said the child.

Jerónimo looked around at the assembled people.

'We don't want to deceive you. We don't want to talk to you about God and angels. We're fighting for these kids. We don't want them working but in school and have a life like kids should,' he said, visibly moved.

I left the gathering and went to the mayor's house. The Chief was still asleep. The big woman had prepared a hot breakfast for him and was waiting in the patio chatting with one of our men.

'How long will you be here in town?' she asked me. I noticed my comrade's uneasy expression, and caught on that she had asked him the same question.

'He'll decide,' I said, nodding my head toward the room where the Chief was sleeping.

'My husband is probably worried to death out there in the jungle,' she said in a soft voice that you wouldn't expect from such a large, strong woman.

Darío came toward us. He was fingering a roll of bills, and showed them to the woman.

'We need food and clothing,' he said to her. 'We're going to pay you for everything.'

'We'll do all we can,' said the woman.

I went into the room where the Chief was asleep. I stood before him and studied him carefully. New, deep wrinkles had begun to ridge his face. I felt admiration for him again. His beard, which he always kept clean, could barely cover the traces of pain and fatigue. He slept soundly, every now and again tossing his head nervously. His hands, fair and delicate despite the rough campaign life he was living, rested like soft doves at his sides. I said to myself, "For a man like that our sacrifice is worth it."

Without me making the slightest sound, he awoke suddenly but was not startled. He sat up and said with a rueful grin, 'I guess I was tired; I fell asleep.'

'There's no hurry. They're bringing you some breakfast,' I said.

The big woman came into the room to offer him his breakfast. The Chief accepted with a smile. I thought I glimpsed in the woman's eyes a little less admiration for the man to whom she gave a few hours' rest in her house.

After the Chief ate his breakfast, we went over to the town assembly. On the way over, we filled him in on what had happened.

'So they're baffled, too,' he said smiling, and added, 'Some chase; the hunters arrive before the prey and come back afterward—it's a circle!'

In the assembly, everybody was talking in a low voice. Apparently they were no longer afraid of the shabby, bearded men who smiled at them. Jerónimo was showing the boy a gadget on his gun. Everybody quieted down when they saw us come in and ascend a sort of mound, from where the Chief would speak.

'Good morning,' the Chief said with a wave of greeting.

Nobody answered. The teacher eagerly moved closer; this was one show he didn't want to miss.

'I thank you for the information you have offered my comrades; it will be useful to us,' the Chief began his speech. 'We do not want to cause you any inconvenience; we will leave as soon as we have rested up and provide ourselves with what we need. There will be no theft; of this you may be assured. Everything we take in the way of food or clothing is to be paid for. I tolerate no abuse in my comrades. We are fighting for justice, and we will never start committing any injustice. We are fighting for you, although this may seem strange to you. We want a human and dignified way of life for you and your children and for all Bolivians. We want this land to benefit those who are born in it, those who work and live in it, not foreign capitalists. You lead a miserable life: you have no electricity, you have no roads to the city, you lack drinking water, you do not have a good school, your children cannot study an honorable profession if they so wish, you lack hygiene and medical care if you get sick, and many other things. All this we can get for you with your help. And to all this you have a right, because you are human beings, and it shall be yours if you firmly make up your mind to obtain it. We do not ask you to face the army; that's what we are here for. But you can fight for a new life by making sure that the army will get no help from you, by not giving them food, information. . . .' The Chief fell silent for a moment. The crowd listened in silence, revealing neither approval nor disapproval of what they heard. Only the teacher seemed satisfied, but I kept having the uncomfortable feeling of not being able to say exactly why he seemed so.

A baby a few months old began to cry loudly. His mother rocked it nervously; she was obviously afraid of attracting attention. She was young and pretty. The Chief smiled and told her to give him some milk. The woman covered her breast with her shawl and began to nurse the baby.

The Chief began again, 'We are fighting here far from our homes, in great discomfort. We are not fighting for ourselves, but for the future of all of you. We come with no false promises. You will have enough power to reject us if we do not make good. We're not threatening you either; you have complete freedom to choose, only think about everything I've told you. The world must now be either with the Revolution or against the Revolution. The Revolution does not give you a little plot of land that you will not know how to till afterward; it means organizing production scientifically so that each one receives according to his needs and according to his contribution to the welfare of all. Revolution means guaranteeing the right to human dignity, so that no man will ever, for any reason whatsoever, be looked upon or held as inferior to another. We are all of us equal in birth and death; we should also be equal in life. Revolution means giving man his own destiny, making him the creator of himself. . . . I want to close this talk, which I am sure many of you will never forget for the rest of your lives, by stressing this: let them say what they want about us, about the guerrillas, but this alone is true: we have freely taken upon ourselves our historic responsibility with no private economic interest. We bring you the hope of a new world, not the perpetuation of outmoded systems. We do not fight for ourselves, but for the children of this crossbreed America whom we will perhaps never see. Many of us are going to die in this struggle, but you should never forget that if we do, it is in order to bring to you, bestow upon you, a human life worthy of every person living in the twentieth century.'

The Chief became silent and raised his hand to his forehead in weariness. I was afraid he'd faint. Nobody gave any sign of consent or reproach. Only we, his comrades, were moved. The silence lasted several minutes. The Chief went over to Darío and murmured something in his ear. The latter stepped forward and spoke to the people.

'If you have any questions, we will be most happy to answer them. Please don't be afraid of us. We're armed, not to attack you or to defend ourselves from you, but to forestall any more moves by the army.'

The teacher, as I expected, was raring to start talking and came forward with his right hand raised.

'The men in the army told us that you're not revolutionaries but just a regular invasion force who come here following the orders of foreign powers to enslave our Country; I'd like you to clear that up,' he said in an even voice and with his usual cryptic expression of mockery, scorn, or friendship.

'I'm going to answer that,' said the Chief. 'You, so I am told, are the schoolmaster, is that right?'

'Yes I am.'

'Very well. Who are the fathers of this Country, Bolivia?'"

'Bolívar and Sucre.'

'Of course. Now, . . . were they born in Upper Peru . . . ?'

'No! They were Venezuelans,' interrupted the professor.

'That's correct. This must sound like one of your classroom quizzes. But the men who freed us from Spanish domination were Americans. We are all Americans. All the peoples of America must unite together against Yankee imperialism and against the capitalists.'

The Chief waited for another question. One of the teen-age boys stepped forward. 'He says you're Communists and you don't believe in God,' he said, becoming pale.

The Chief didn't answer immediately. He looked up at the sky. The sun had risen until it shone almost directly over our heads.

'Is there a priest in this town?' he asked, after lowering his eyes and looking at the boy.

'No,' said the teacher, because the boy dared not reply.

'Do you receive help from the Church every day, or at least whenever you want it? I am sure you do not. The priests are all in the cities, where there are fat donations and there are clean-cut people to invite them out to dinner. Coming here would be too much of a sacrifice. The army, which kills miners and supports injustice, has its chaplains, but here God has not even sent one. In our opinion, we must first fight for a better deal here on earth, which is where we are actually hungry, where we suffer life's wants. We leave the problem of heaven and God up to the conscience of each person. We wish to insure work, bread, and freedom for the person who is in need of these things; religion is a personal question for the conscience.

The boy wore a neutral expression; he didn't seem to be satisfied. No one asked any more questions. The meeting broke up at the Chief's command. We all began the job of providing ourselves with food and clothing. At sundown I went out to relieve one of the guards we had stationed on a hill at the entrance to the town. He asked me about the days events. I told him, without going into details.

At dawn the following day we left the village without making the slightest sound, and nobody saw us depart.

14　We came up to a fairly deep river. Some airplanes were flying around the area, so we had to lie low for almost the whole day. At nightfall, a comrade from José's unit came up to meet us. Their unit was being pursued by the army, so they were retreating to the north, where the jungle was heavier. Somebody had betrayed them, a guy by the name of Rubén, a volunteer recruited from the tin mines of Siglo Veinte. They had fought two skirmishes with the army, and fell into an ambush. Apparently the army was following out a definite, well-planned timetable. The comrade was tired. His trousers were all torn up, and he wore only a pair of battered sandals to protect his bleeding feet. After he had rested up, I went over to ask him about José.

'The kid from Cochabamba?' he asked.

'Yes,' I replied.

'Well, he's dead,' he said without even looking at me.

15   We ran across an old woman and her granddaughter along a trail. The girl was about eleven and seemed very bright. They kept goats and lived in a nearby farmhouse. The old lady agreed to let the Chief spend the night or a part of it in her house. We bought four goats from her to butcher. She would accept any amount of money and gave the impression that she wasn't aware of its true value. She informed us that the army was moving about nearby. We had the impression she was hiding something, but she was the only person we could trust, for a price. We all thought it over and came to the decision we'd cross the deep river upstream and hole up in the heavy jungle. The army wouldn't dare go in there. The Chief was worse than ever and could no longer stand up. We asked the old lady to get us a mule. She said she'd bring it to us

at night; she'd go to a friend's house to get it. We let her go, but even though the little girl and her flock remained with us, we still had some misgivings.

She returned late at night with a pretty fair mule. She suggested that we leave at dawn, since the army patrol didn't show any signs of being around. We asked her to guide us to the ford, and offered to pay her well. She said that she couldn't walk fast and that she was very tired from her journey to get the mule. However, she offered her granddaughter's help on condition that we paid her before leaving. Darío and I made all the arrangements, because the Chief had taken a bad turn and had a high fever.

I couldn't sleep before our departure. I wrote these lines. I began to think of Laura.

"Laura, will I ever see you again?" I ask myself.

The Captain wiggles his belly with joy. He scratches the back of his neck. He tugs down the visor on his cap and chuckles to himself. The old lady looks at him and can't figure out what he's laughing at. And the Captain says, Hot shit, at last I'm going to get a few of the breaks. Then he talks to the old lady, but we can't hear anything they're saying. So we're dying of curiosity and pass the time watching the closed door of the shack the Captain calls his "General Headquarters." At last the two come out; the old lady first, with a look on her face like an innocent virgin, and then the Captain, with a big, shit-eating grin spread all over his. The Captain tells her, Go back home, do everything I told you, and don't worry about a thing. Then he points to Camba and says, We've got a hell of a good scout to guide us to the spot. And the old lady waddles off without so much as turning her head. Okay, get ready to move out with combat equipment; we're going to get those hairy bandits this time, as sure as God's in heaven. We pull out. The Captain follows behind everybody else and tries not to let on how glad he is. He has to hold back an urge to sing. I'm thinking, Parrot baby, Divine Providence is setting things up so I can keep my word and make good what I promised you. That Camba has the eyes of a panther; he can make out the trail even at night. We're all going along, but fearing that maybe it's just another trick of the guerrillas. But if it is, I'm thinking, the old lady sure as hell isn't getting away with it.

When it's dark, the jungle's scary. It gives you the creeps even after you make up your mind not to think about being afraid and about dying. We've been marching along this still, black trail for over three hours, and then when we're ready to drop from exhaustion and fear, Camba halts and says, There it is, and tells me to inform the Captain. I go to the rear with Camba's message. The Captain's sweating like hell, but manages pretty well to cover up how tired he is. He says, Okay, everybody hold up here, cuz we're going to cross the river. I know it's hard at night, but it's just one sacrifice more we have to make to save our Country from those fucking invaders. We're all scared and looking around; but you can't see what you're looking out for, you can't know it. It's black and dangerous. By now our eyes are used to the darkness of the jungle, and we can make out the trees on the other bank. The water stands out plainer, like it always does; it looks like dark silver. But how can you know for sure that there's just trees over there? Crossing the river's going to be long and tough. Ever since that old lady came, our fate's been shaping up out there, and it might catch up with us tonight. She comes right into the camp and picks me out to tell she wants to talk with the Captain. Everyone laughs and says he's got no time for old ladies; to get into the "General Headquarters" you have to be forty and under. I tell them, Shut up, you dumb bastards, cuz I think we may all owe something to this lady before we're through. She might be a good omen. Camba squeezes most of the water out of his pants and says how he could go for a cigarette now. I'm thinking I could, too, but it's the Captain's express order, so what we'd like stays a wish. I start bringing up Parrot in my mind, and naturally Filly. Parrot's asking me about her. I tell him, You shithead, you're on the make even up there in heaven. *Filly's really something special; she's a woman who puts out more than anybody else in town.* I feel real proud when the Captain puts his hand on my shoulder and says, "You did great, soldier," music to my ears, like when I hear "Filly." "If all goes well, your furlough and promotion are a sure bet." I also feel real proud of my serious look. The Captain's treating the old lady like she was the Queen of Sheba, and he says to us, Men, all we can do is trust her. We're playing for keeps this time like never before. Jelly-Belly's running around sticking each guy in a different place, according to all that stuff he had to learn when he was a cadet. Camba's the only guy who knows how to cover up footprints; I hope he's damn careful not to miss one, cuz if he does, those fucking guerrillas'll shoot our ass off. Without a second thought. This time they're not going to spare anybody. The old lady must be talking to the guerrillas already, trying to talk them into it, like kids. And here we are, ready and waiting, not even blowing a blade of grass. Like the Captain said, You bastards only have permission to blink, or piss in your pants if you feel like it—but do it without a sound.

The Chief dozes; his head bobs in rhythm to the gait of his mule. The men move in single file spaced five to ten paces apart. The girl was walking at Darío's side, but she is more jittery now and runs on ahead. Every step takes me farther away from you, Laura. The trail rose steeply through rocks and underbrush, then abruptly fell into a valley following a bare ravine. Down below shone the river. This is it, Parrot; it'll more than make up to you for what happened between Filly and me. The girl halted when she came to the top of the hill.

'My grandma said I should only come this far and then go back,' the girl says, looking at the water flowing at the bottom of the slope.

'But we want to know where the ford is,' says Darío.

She continues to stare at the river, then points down. 'There it is; it's real shallow.'

Javier comes up to Darío and the girl. The Chief follows behind on the mule. The bastards are getting near their last stand, Parrot; I can see 'em coming, like little specks over on the hill. The Captain says we should let 'em come down, and he'll fire the first shot. I'm praying, please, dear Virgin of Copacabana. But my heart's going faster than my prayer. Javier smiles at the girl.

'She says the ford's at the foot of the hill. She doesn't want to go down,' says Darío.

Javier looks over at the Chief and repeats what Darío said.

'Yeah, okay,' the Chief mumbles, fighting his fever, failing to understand Javier's words.

Darío looks around suspiciously. Everything remains quiet. We're all shivering, Parrot, with the cold and nerves and seeing the guerrillas stalling. "Looks like they're shitting in their pants," says the Captain, and tells us be sure not to move.

'Cross the river with me and then you can go back to your grandma,' says Darío.

'My grandma said I should go back and not cross the river.' Her voice is close to tears.

The Chief grits his teeth. Hang on, Parrot, they gotta come down sometime. Waiting's getting on my nerves. The Captain says they're arguing with the kid, the granddaughter.

'Let her go; she's done enough,' Javier says.

Darío answers, 'I don't know; something's funny.'

Chaco looks at me and comes over. "Problems?" he whispers. "I don't know; something's funny," says Darío, looking at the girl, who has begun to whimper. I look at the Chief, shivering on his mule. I go over and take his hand. He opens his eyes and smiles down at me. You'd think those hairy bastards would start coming down to cross the river.

'Do we cross, Chief?' I ask.

'Sure,' he mutters.

'Let me cross with the girl first,' says Darío.

She starts to cry harder. 'But my grandma's going to whip me.'

Thinking back in the midst of all this is like a breath of fresh air. But, hell, it doesn't last long, cuz then your conscience stings you, like a poisonous caterpillar, telling me I shouldn't have done it to her. Could Filly be hoping for something? Making plans? Dammit, be careful; it's something that can be worked out later. Filly's dangerous; like a cliff, but with a fresh meadow down at the bottom running cool water and the honey of love.

It keeps getting lighter all the time, Parrot. We're like stones; nobody talks or moves. I haven't forgotten our friendship, Parrot, and I'm just itching to jump up yelling, and shoot and kill. The Chief mumbles something incoherent and blinks his eyes. He is sweating and shivering. Weird little shapes, all smiles and glittering in bright colors, surround his mule. One of them puts out something like a tentacle to straighten his clothes and utters consoling sounds he cannot understand. He answers, trying to copy its actions. The other two creatures weave their gleaming tentacles together. With an effort, the Chief manages to make out a fourth shape, as tiny as a slug. He turns to speak to it, but when it hears him it makes shrill noises that hurt his ears.

The day begins to sketch itself out over the hills, a pale line beyond the black mass of the mountain ridge.

'I'm going to give you a present,' Darío says to the little girl, taking her hand, and tells me, 'Go back and tell the comrades to wait until the girl gets back before going down.'

Chaco takes the reins of the mule, humming a tune from his home town. I'm thinking I may never see you again, Laura, and walk on.

Actually, when you think of it, Parrot, the guys who really should be jumpy are the three the Captain stuck right up where the guerrillas are talking. They can probably even see the whiskers of the guy on the mule. He's probably their chief. Chiefs are always like that; they ride comfortable and safe so they can get away fast— but that's not what's going to happen this time. Yeah, not this time. The Captain's a sly fox, Parrot. Right before he put us here, he told me now's the time when we're going to pay back those guys who killed you. He was smiling, thinking out loud and rubbing his hands, planning it out. He offered the old lady a big fat reward. The three soldiers at the top of the hill can hear the girl whining. They gently squeeze their machine-gun triggers. Ten soldiers lie hidden behind the rocks along the wide path that goes down to the river. Yes sir, Parrot, the Captain was real cagey and thought of everything. I feel like I'm forsaking you; I speak to the comrades and they ask me what's wrong. The Captain whispers, "Everybody quiet and don't shoot until they pass the ford." We're all watching. He says they won't cross with the old lady's granddaughter. Who wants innocent people to get killed?

The girl refuses to move.
'Here's fifty pesos,' Darío says to her; 'get yourself a nice pair of shoes.'
She stops crying and takes the money. 'But my grandma told me not to cross the river,' she says as she begins to descend the slope.
Two of them have started, Parrot; they're sliding down the gully. The Captain says, Not yet, men, hang on. The mule stirs uneasily.
'Shh, old girl,' Chaco says.
Filly, I promise I'm going to get even with Parrot's murderer. "Did you see who killed my Parrot, his murderer?" she blubbered, pressing her tits into my chest. Parrot, I swear I'll get him. At first I'm not doing anything, not even thinking of anything, because Filly's yours. But she's the one who's insisting; who wouldn't want her when she starts rubbing herself up against you? So I'm sweating and I squeeze her arm and she puts her face against mine. And I'm giving in fast, Parrot, because Filly's a real woman, stacked, her body's as soft as a sponge, and her skin's smooth, made for feeling. I know she's just a little whore, but she sure knows how to give you a good time. I swear I'll get at least one of them, Filly baby, just to even things up. Now you're my friend; because you were a friend of his, she says, you're my friend. She caught me off guard and she's making me want to show her my manhood and I let myself go and give in. And my hand starts rubbing her

127

soft flesh. The two people are already standing on the bank, Parrot.

'One of them's the girl,' whispers the Captain.

"The dirty bastards," I say to myself. Well, maybe that's her fate, the way things are supposed to work out for her.

The man picks the girl up in his arms and wades into the river. The water is warmer than the air. I leave the group and go over to the Chief and Chaco, and ask if Darío and the girl got across the ford.

'They're crossing now,' Chaco says, nodding his head toward the river.

'How's the Chief getting along?' I ask.

'Still got a fever. As soon as we get to the jungle, he can rest and we can fix him up.'

'The comrades are pretty cool,' I say.

'Great.'

Darío comes to the halfway mark and stops. He thinks he hears the murmur of a voice from the other bank.

'Are you afraid, too?' the girl asks.

'Be quiet,' he answers.

On the far bank, a tall, dense tangle rises up. Nothing can be distinguished in it under the dull glow of dawn. The birds are beginning to hop and flutter around in the foliage. "An entire army could be waiting for us over there," Darío says to himself. Yet his ears hear no suspicious noise, his eyes detect no movement that could betray a human presence. The girl watches him with a fear close to tears.

'Don't worry, honey. Everything's okay,' Darío says with a smile, and continues to wade across.

They're shitting in their pants, as the Captain put it so well. He stopped, Parrot; he almost threw the girl in the water and opened up on us. That would have spoiled the Captain's big ambush; all our waiting for nothing. My conscience keeps bringing up the Filly thing. I guess because I want to justify what I did. *But Filly's a woman, a real woman. Before anything else she's a woman, Parrot, so what's a guy going to do?* She had me so I'd do and think whatever she wanted me to. She presses up against me and I'm looking into her eyes as close as you can get. Then I sigh and she looks at me and blows on my nose. And the room's warm and I'm thinking I'd like to relax and have a little fun before going out again to chase those damn guerrillas. And Parrot, she's getting real horny and wants it bad. And I want it, too, when I feel her giving in to the slightest touch of my fingers. You know how it is, Parrot, because we were buddies and always screwing around together when we met her. The guerrilla left the girl on the beach, and he's coming close to our hiding place. He's holding his gun ready. He looks around, but can't tell we're here. I have to bite my lip to keep from blasting him right now, Parrot, and keeping that promise.

'He put the girl down, and he's going up to where the jungle starts,' Chaco says.

'I'm going to tell the comrades to start moving,' says Javier.

'Better wait for Darío's sign. When he gets a hunch, he's seldom wrong.'

'All right,' says Javier.

I must go back to you someday. It doesn't matter how, but I must, Laura. You must never forget me.

Darío approaches the nearest clump of undergrowth and throws a stone. He waits a moment and parts the branches a little with the muzzle of his automatic. Nobody there. The first rays of morning filter through the dense foliage and strike the ground like a wistful memory of the sun. Darío turns toward the girl, who is whimpering again.

'It's okay, now; go back to your grandma,' he tells her, patting her chin. 'I won't forget how much you helped us, my little friend.'

She turns and quickly recrosses the river. Darío signals to the men on the other side. Chaco starts down, tugging at the reins of the mule. The rest follow.

That was a close call. That guerrilla bastard was looking right at us, but he couldn't decide if we were here or not. He came to within two steps. Parrot, I saw the whiskers on his chin. It was hard to keep from letting him have it right then. Nobody moved an inch. I don't think the Captain breathed or even moved his eyelids. Now the guy's on the beach, signaling to the ones on the top. Here comes one now, pulling the mule by the reins. The mule starts to slide. The Chief feels like he's slipping down into a whirlpool. He struggles to open his eyes; the light of early day stings him mercilessly. He can barely see the gleaming shape twisting its formless head and gaping its friendship with its huge mouth. One of its tentacles stretches out to touch his sinking vessel. Yet the friendly gestures of his strange companion reassure him, and he feels not the slightest fear.

The two are already halfway down the hill. We're going to bust a gut if they don't hurry. Just wait, Parrot baby; trust in the Virgin of Copacabana, because I'm going to get at least two of the guys that got you.

We're all moving again. Darío made sure it's safe. They'll never catch us if we make it over to the thick jungle, because it stretches all the way to the Amazon. I have an urge to write you a letter, Laura. I stop to take the notebook out of my pack. I'll compose it in my mind and write it down on our next stop. But this letter you'll get only when we meet again. I'm sure, after we reach that bank, everything will work itself out and I'll find my way back to you. Laura, that bank is a symbol of hope.

Am I in love with her? Like hell. I absolutely refuse to think anything of the sort. It's just the loneliness and war nerves. It's crazy to try making any plans. Love is pure intentions, anyhow. Like the fresh smile of a girl who hasn't been out whoring around. But . . . could I be? Snap out of it! Hell no! I refuse to think about it any more.

The men slowly descend the rugged slope. The sun shines in the distance, its sphere just peeking over the jagged line of mountains. Chaco has arrived at the shore. The mule lowers his head and drinks. Chaco looks up at the men behind and tells them to hurry. I wade into the river and feel its caressing warmth rising as I go deeper. I see Darío still moving along the beach on the other side. Now we're all in midstream. The Chief rides in the middle because of the slow pace of his mule. The girl stops when she sees the three soldiers; they tell her to run home. They are under cover on a high rock and waiting, watching the dust settle down on the slope.

Darío continues to walk up the beach. He stops short when he notices odd footprints in the sand. He follows them to a hollow in an enormous rotten tree trunk. He cocks his gun. When he is in front of the hollow, he looks back; all the men are already crossing the wide ford. A reflection on top of the opposite hill catches his eye. In a fraction of a second it is all clear.

'Back! Get back!' he shouts and fires at the hollow.

The Chief jumps at the sound of the shots. He sees shimmering figures bobbing up and down in the water at his feet. Rapid little flashes pop from the metallic extensions of their tentacles. Some of them surround him and try to communicate something to him with a desperation he cannot understand. Everything is a maelstrom of lights and waving tentacles sticking out to steer his vessel away from the glittering vortex.

And we're really letting them have it. I'm firing, killing. This is just what I've been waiting for after hours without moving. I see a guy pulling his Chief's mule trying to hide somewhere, yelling and firing at everything and all confused. I aim cool and squeeze off a shot and he falls into the water. I'm killing and raging like a nut, but cool because I'm safe. The Captain's saying, This is what those sonofabitches got coming. Everyone shouting and shooting and the empty shells falling all over. The hairy bastards are going in circles trying to escape; those goddam Communist traitors are trying to get away, but they're not going anywhere. From up above the machine guns are sweeping the river. Christ! This is really pretty to watch, Parrot baby; it's pretty, not forgetting, seeing the bullets splash in the water, splitting the stones, hitting bodies so the blood comes out and makes the river red. The mule's squealing, with wounds all over, and the man riding him looks like he's waking up from some dream, gaping all around him, his hands up, trying to throw off an imaginary weight. The Captain says, Get that guy alive; he's their Chief, but he falls dead because the guys above didn't hear him and keep shooting, happier than hell that we're winning.

One last, pointless shot. The soldiers remain motionless for a long minute in their hiding places. The morning breeze wafts away the smell of cordite. The silence is total, barely broken by the murmur of water lapping the shore and the corpses.

We all jump at the Captain's voice giving orders. We have to pick up the bodies. We get into the water. I grab the body of a hairy guy with his whole face a mess and his chest riddled with bullets.

The soldiers recover the bodies of the guerrillas and line them up in a row face up on the beach. The Captain starts counting them.

'Fourteen!' he exclaims.

'Then, one's missing,' says the Sergeant.

'We have to keep searching. Take six soldiers. Go downstream along both shores until you locate him. We have to wipe them all out. That way we won't have any more headaches in this Country,' says the Captain, rubbing his hands.

The man moves his head. His cheek rests on the sand. He opens his eyes and watches the water breaking against a rock, raising greenish foam. He tries to get up, but a sharp pain in his shoulder prevents him from lifting his body. "I'm wounded," he thinks.

Four soldiers walk along one shore, three others with the Sergeant along the other. They move slowly, carefully searching the surface of the river and the sand on the beach. The water seems motionless, as if it stood still. A few fisher birds fly in low circles beyond the soldiers. One of them stops on the beach and picks up a dark, wet object and shows it to the Sergeant.

'It's a notebook,' says the Sergeant, trying to thumb through the wet pages, which tear at the slightest pull. The ink has run on some of the pages, making them impossible to read.

I want to move my fingers, but they don't obey.

I'm trying to crawl into the shade. The sun's too hot for me to be lying on the broiling sand. After much pain and effort, I discover it's my shoulder that's hurt, shattered by a bullet. The blood keeps oozing out. After I manage to crawl into the shade, I rest a moment and sit down. My arm hangs like a useless hunk of meat, like a branch suspended by a thread from a tree, ready to fall off. I've lost lots of blood and I'm losing more. I look back and see a dark streak stretching from the riverbank to my hiding place. "If the soldiers come, it won't take long to find me," I say to myself, as I take my shirt off and make a tourniquet to stanch or at least slow down the bleeding.

The Sergeant sits down on a rock and begins to read the notebook. I'm thinking of you and Filly, Parrot. I made you both a promise in the name of our friendship, and I've kept it, Parrot, and I'll keep it still better. It's like a beautiful fever that's got into my veins and's warming up my heart with a nice little glow. I should be the one to get the guy we're after. To soothe my conscience over the Filly deal; but hell, I'm a man same as you, Parrot, same as everybody else. And the Filly's a woman who doesn't want us men to forget she's a woman and what she puts out. The Sarge's happier than a pig in shit, cuz he's found some clues to go on.

The cloth becomes soggy with blood. A bit of my strength has come back and I go down to the water and wet down my shirt and make a tourniquet. Little by little, the blood stops running. I take a stick and try to cover up my footprints and the trickle of blood. I'm getting terribly tired. I start out for my hide-out. My head's spinning. I feel as if I'm going to pass out. I make it back and lie down in the shade.

The four soldiers have spotted an object floating in the river. One of them leaves his clothes on the bank and dives in. The others signal to those on the other shore.

'What is it?' yells the Sergeant.

'I don't know, Sarge; looks like a pack,' replies one of the soldiers.

The soldier comes back to the shore carrying a wet pack.

"It's a pack, Sarge,' says one of the soldiers.

'Bring it here,' orders the Sergeant.

Could I be in love? The thought keeps nagging me. Actually, you could be in love and still not be sure about it and could even be tired of thinking about it. Real love, I guess, should make you accept the doubt as well as the happiness. But it's all for something worth while. It's for what love gains, deserves. But no, I'm trying to sell myself on this. Filly's a woman, and love picks the woman for the man. And that's it. But my conscience? Hell, why should it bother me? It's an intrusion from outside.

I recall the ambush. I picture the Chief again, caught in the midst of his fever, struggling to comprehend what's going on around him. I rush forward to make him jump into the water; when I'm just a few steps away, he throws his hands up into the air. They seem to rise up to the sky and then plunge to the bottom of the river. I stand bewildered, while bullets whistle around my ears and the soldiers' shouts deafen the air. I fire a burst into the bank and then duck under, submerging my head and body, but holding my automatic out of the water. When I run out of air, I come up and try to keep firing, but a dizziness in my brain pushes me down into a bottomless dark void. "God almighty, I've had it," I say to myself.

The Sergeant opens the pack and removes the contents, laying them out in a row on the beach. He finds a scapular among some dirty old rags. He holds it up to show the soldiers and laughs. 'I'll be damned; he believes in God and the Virgin,' he says.

The soldiers on the other shore start shouting. The Sergeant gets up and cups his hand around his ear.

'What are they saying?' he asks.

I answer, Something about an automatic, Sarge, and cartridge belts, I think. He says, Shit! that's great; that's music to my ears, what do y' say? I say so, too, only more so. I'm watching the river, Parrot, with its water as muddy as life—it's not crystal clear, but it's not as black as soot, either.

I've made it up again. I've stopped bleeding. I think I can walk now. At last I can think about getting out of here. It's impossible to cover up all my tracks. I'll head downstream. I don't know if I can get far enough away before the soldiers show up looking for survivors. No one else could possibly have gotten out of that slaughter alive. The loneliness in the middle of the jungle is terrible.

'Here's a trace of blood, Sarge,' says a soldier.

'He tried to erase it. The blood's pretty dry,' says the Sergeant.

The soldiers work silently. The Sergeant orders the ones on the other side to cross over on the nearby ford.

'Sergeant!' a soldier calls and hands him a piece of bloody cloth.

'Where?' asks the Sergeant.

'In this hole,' says the soldier.

The Sergeant says, I reckon this hairy little bastard's had it right down to the last hair on his little red ass, and he smiles that fiendish grin of his that means he knows what he's doing. He asks me, Do you know what's downstream? I say, Well, Sarge, you can get up pretty close to that path that . . . By damn, you're right, he cuts in. His eyes are brighter than glowing coals. I know what he's thinking, and it both scares and excites me. He hands me the notebook and tells me to read a certain page carefully, and wants to know if I have any imagination left. My eyes don't believe they're seeing what they're seeing. My blood wants to pop out of my veins with the joy I'm feeling. The Sergeant asks if there's a short cut to the farmhouse we're starting to get ideas about. Camba says there is: by the short cut the house is three leagues away; downstream by river it's twice as far. The Sarge's laughing and winking at me and says, We got the bastard. This is my big chance, Parrot baby.

The river elbows in a right angle, then widens out and forms a shallow ford. A path descends from the hill to the ford.

I've got to keep on going like this. Like this? The Rector rises and tells me, Your mind's already made up. I'm running, and Mario's after me. We broke one. God almighty. I should make it before it gets dark. The horses are coming and we're running away. I broke it, Mom. The Rector looks at me and says, It's the only thing you could do. "The choice is entirely yours . . . and so is its justification," he says. One of the horses is jet black and he's about to overtake us; Mario's laughing and crying at the same time. We can't run any more; the black horse jumps over us, and the Rector saves us. The sun's up there, but it's getting weak. God almighty.

Damn you, Camba, I told you to tell me where it is; I can move faster. Our fast trot is making us tired, and the sun doesn't hide behind any cloud; it just keeps glaring. Camba says I look like I've gone nuts. I'm not nuts; it's just to get even; it's the promise I made to God and the Virgin of Copacabana in the name of my friendship with Parrot, to make up for what they did to him. It was wrong, and my conscience is telling me I gotta even things up and pay them back. Camba's a guy who doesn't buy any of this; he doesn't give a damn about friendship and about standing by Parrot after we've been friends so long. We're sweating and panting, even though the sun's only got half a face left peeking over the horizon. Camba says, "We finally made it, friend." We should see the ford and the path from over there. The house is on the other side in the middle of the banana and chestnut trees, he says; his breath's coming in pants and shows he's had it. Damn sweat's getting in my eyes.

The canoe shoots around the bend, then slows down where the river broadens out. The man paddles laboriously to the shore.

'I see him, Camba.'

The Rector laughs and embraces Dad and they're both agreed that it's better this way. "It's what we would have done in his place," they chant in unison. Mario and I look at each other. The horses are galloping across the field at us, their hoofs striking sparks against the stones. Thank God the sun's going down at last. God almighty. Gotta get there before the horses run me down. Juana screams, too. My mother sees the horses and holds out her arms to me. I don't get it. This is the end. This is the path, here. Juana and Carlos watch me playing with the hobby horse and want to play, too. "We all justify our life by our acts," says the theology professor.

'I have to make it before it gets dark! . . .'

'Yeah, down there; it's a canoe.'

Laura's all alone now, waiting in the house as usual. My fever's letting up, thank God. I'll make it. But what about the horses? It's only a . . . a. . . .

'I'll be damned; a canoe with a man in it.'

'Yeah, there's a man in it.'

'Mr. Rector, I've come to . . . to. . . .'

'Come right in, Javier, come right in.'

'The bastard's wounded; he can't handle it.'

'This is it, Parrot baby.'

The soldier takes his cap off and wipes his face with a dirty handkerchief.

'I'll wait for him by the path. You go on up to the house and arrest the old man and his daughter. The Sarge'll be down by the river later.'

'Tonight, again, it'll be like the other nights, Laura.'

The other soldier hesitates. 'You're too fired up. It'd be better to take him alive. That's my opinion.'

'Juana, you have to come tonight, because. . . .'

'Get up to that goddam house!' says the soldier, tightening his grip on his gun menacingly.

'Actually, going to Mass doesn't mean a thing to me any more, or kneeling before the Blessed Sacrament. It's all so cold, Carlos.'

'But the guy's wounded; it's not combat any more.'

'I'll come back, Laura. I promise you. I'm. . . .'

'God damn it, it's me, not you, that has to square things up.'

'God is encountered in a right will and in justice; I believe . . .'

Camba turns and starts up reluctantly. After walking a way he stops and looks back. 'It's wrong,' he cries in a loud voice.

'Bullshit! How about them killing our guys?' the soldier snarls, and hefts his weapon threateningly.

'I'm tired, Laura. . . . I've tramped across an entire jungle, and . . .'

The white horse is for you, Carlos, and the black one for you, Laura, and the other one for . . . The man gets out of the canoe. As he steps on land, a terrible pain jerks his body. His breathing is feverish. "I think I'm going out of my head." I'm laying for you all alone, you dirty, bearded bastard, using the same strategy you used to kill Parrot. That's right; it's Parrot's buddy who's going to even things up. That's right, Parrot's and Filly's, *because she's a woman and I fell for her. Did I really? Shit! Filly does what you want as long as you pay her, paid her cash . . . that's all she ever was. But it's all over. So? So what? How the hell can you think of the future in a spot like this. Even your own. Okay, so I've still got ideas about her; that's what I get for having her and taking what she was only too willing to put out.*

"Is everything lost?" the man asks himself as he drags his body along the narrow path, uphill.

EPILOGUE

Javier:

"Is everything lost?" you will ask yourself over and over again as you drag your body up the path like a sluggish reptile. In your silent pause, your fever and delirium will have left you. The bandage, the tourniquet you tied on, will have slipped off and the blood will gush out again. You will not even have the strength to call out her name, Laura's name, and you will also be afraid that the sound will give you away to the soldiers, who you know will be in close pursuit. Your weariness, weakness, and excitement will make you pause for a moment. You will turn your head around and see the track you made, oddly visible in the darkness which will already have settled over everything that surrounds you. Your fresh blood will mix with mud and trace a gloomy streak of brightness in the path. You will feel yourself the source

147

of that stream, and you will go on feeding that brightness in the path, giving of yourself, giving up yourself, only to be changed little by little (as told in ancient myths) into the giddy murmur of a cool stream. You will reach out your hand and touch the mass made with your own blood; that "slime" you will feel as your own, as what you are already becoming, the clay you already are. You will remember (in that, your moment, untimed by clock) Carlos, the seminary, your parents, Juana, the only girl you could seduce, the lofty ideal that brought you to this wild, distant place. Caught up in the final frenzy, you will also remember your Chief, that great man no longer on earth. You will struggle to find some comfort; then your fingers will again begin to toil, clutching plants to drag your body up the path. You will have to close your eyes, for you can no longer hold your head up or keep your face off the ground. When you get to the top you will again open your eyes and see a shape draw near (by now everything has become formless shapes) and you will wish to smile, thanking God you're seeing Laura. But your smile will freeze and will be shocked into a grimace, for the shape standing over you will hold a metal object. You will see his weapon with astonishing clarity, like a *collage* in a shadowy frame, hung before you by a great artist. You will shut your eyes and imagine you hear the explosion of the cartridge and then feel its projectile tug you away from life. Still you will weep silently for Laura, for your aloneness, for the world you are leaving. But you will hear no shot, only the sobs of someone saying, "Brother," not knowing you can no longer hear. Javier, you can no longer hear.

Laura:

You will be calming your father as the soldier tells you to hurry and flee to the jungle, that he will bear all the risk. You will ask, and your whole life will be in the question, if anyone has survived. The soldier will say everybody is dead and the Sergeant's coming down the river with a patrol to burn the house and take everybody prisoner. Your father will try to remain, arguing that he is old and that he is innocent. The soldier will tell you that there will be no mercy for anybody, and, Laura, that even your honor will be in danger. You will take a bundle of two or three articles of clothing that still fit, and leave, thanking the soldier. Your father will continue to ask you to wait for him. While you cross the banana grove, you will place your hand on your belly and know that Javier, the only man you have ever loved, is not dead, that your veins are throbbing with his life, that soon you must feed him with your own milk, clothe him and teach him all you can. As you run on, you will tell this Javier, your *own* Javier, about Javier, about his goodness, about what he was. You will laugh and weep and go on running, holding your bundle of clothes in one hand, and with the other feeling the surge of your joy in the very depth of your womb.

Soldier:

You will stand motionless in the shadows until Camba disappears. When you can no longer see him, you will pray to the Virgin of Copacabana to give you the strength to kill your friend's murderer. As you peer down the darkening path, you will think of Parrot and Filly. You will try to convince yourself that you were a good friend. Your conscience will trouble you over your actions with Filly; after all, she was engaged to your friend. You will try your best to convince yourself that everything will be cleared up when you have killed the guerrilla who is coming up the path and taking such a long time about it. You will be almost sure that Parrot up in heaven will forgive what you did with Filly. Parrot will be at peace with you because you will have kept your word as a friend. You will want to end the wait once and for all and go down to meet the enemy, but some uneasiness in the back of your mind holds you back. You will know this is the thing that keeps you from being completely happy, just as you are about to keep the promise you made as a friend. But without wanting to, you begin to think of the girl in the farmhouse. To get rid of her image you will say under your breath that she is just a dirty camp follower of the guerrillas, but then, without knowing for sure, you will tell yourself she is the lover of the man coming up the path. This will convince you a little more. You will be wrapped in those thoughts when a loud, continuous sound comes from down the path. At first it will be undefined, but then it will be like a broken moan of pain. This moan will make your nerves twitch. You will step out with your carbine cocked to shoot the man you are waiting for. But the man will not come as you thought he would: stumbling along from tree to tree. No, he will be moaning and crawling, dragging his body inch by inch. Then you will know why it took so much time. You will move toward him, pointing your weapon, thinking of Parrot, of his death. When you are three or four steps away, you will halt, and seeing the sad smile of a man about to die, you will lower your gun. Try as you may, you will not be able to think of Parrot or Filly any more, nor pray to the Virgin of Copacabana. You will be standing before him until his smile vanishes, his head drops, and he speaks the girl's name. Then, soldier, you will kneel down by his side and tell him that you want to save him, bind up his wound. You will touch his face; it will be cold and grimy. You will put your ear to his chest and hear but the cold stillness that passes through your ears into the depth of your spirit. You will stand up in dismay, not knowing what to do. Camba will come to meet you and tell you that nobody is in the farmhouse, that they have all fled. From the bottom of the path will drift the sound of your companions coming up with the Sergeant. Camba will repeat that they have all fled. "It's better, God," you will say, and you will begin to weep and hold out your arms to Camba, who will embrace you with the heartiness and understanding of a friend.